William Shakespeare's

Sir Gawain and the Green Knight

In Plain and Simple English

BookCaps™ Study Guides
www.bookcaps.com

Table of Contents

About This Series

The "Classic Retold" series started as a way of telling classics for the modern reader—being careful to preserve the themes and integrity of the original. Whether you want to understand Shakespeare a little more or are trying to get a better grasps of the Greek classics, there is a book waiting for you!

The series is expanding every month. Visit BookCaps.com to see all the books in the series, and while you are there join the Facebook page, so you are first to know when a new book comes out.

Comparative Version

Book One

I

Since Troy's assault and siege, I trow, were
over-past,
To brands and ashes burnt that stately burg at
last,
And he, the traitor proved, for treason that he
wrought,
Was fitly tried and judged, his fortune elsewhere
sought
The truest knight on earth, Aeneas, with his kin,
Who vanquished provinces, and did, as princes,
win
Of all the Western Isles, the wealth and worth
alway;
Rich Romulus to Rome full swift hath ta'en his
way,
First, hath he founded fair that city in his pride
To which he gave his name, it bears it to this
tide;
Ticius doth dwellings found, turning to Tuscany,
And Langobard, a race raised up in, Lombardy.
But Felix Brutus sailed full far, o'er the French
flood,
And on its banks so broad founded Britain, the
good,
in bliss;
Where war nor wonder fail
And ne'er have done, ywis,
Nor shall both bliss and bale
their shifting chances miss.

Since the assault on Troy and its siege were
over,
with that great town reduced to ashes and
flames,
and the one who had been shown to be a traitor
had been properly
tried and judged for his treason, the truest
knight on Earth, Aeneas, with his family,
sought out new provinces and as Princes they
won over
all of the Western Isles, all their wealth and
property;
Rich Romulus went quickly to Rome,
where he founded the great city
to which he gave his name, which it still has
today;
Ticius found a place to live in Tuscany,
and Langobard started a race in Lombardy.
But Felix Brutus sailed the farthest, over the
channel,
and on its broad shores he founded Britain, the
good country, in happiness;
where neither war nor miracles ever end
and never have done, certainly,
and both good and bad fortune
have always swiftly followed each other.

II

And when that baron bold had Britain made, I
trow,
Bold men were bred therein, who loved strife
well enow,
And many a war they waged in those good days
of yore-
Of marvels stern and strange, in this land many
more
Have chanced than otherwhere, since that same
time, I ween-
But of all kings who e'er o'er Britain lords have
been,
Fairest was Arthur all, and boldest, so men tell;

And when that bold baron had established
Britain,
bold men were raised there, who were happy to
fight,
and they fought many wars in those good old
days -
more fearful and amazing things have happened
in this land
than happened elsewhere, since its existence, I
believe -
but of all the kings who have ruled over Britain,
the fairest was Artthur, and the bravest, so men
say;

Therefore I think to shew a venture that befell
In his time, which some men for a sheer wonder
hold,
And strange above all tales that be of Arthur
told.
If ye will list this lay a little while, in sooth,
I'll tell ye as I heard it told in town for truth
with tongue-
As it doth stand, to wit,
In story stiff and strong,
In letters fairly writ,
The land hath known it long.

III

At Camelot lay the King, all on a Christmas-
tide,
With many a lovely lord, and gallant knight
beside,
And of the Table Round did the rich
brotherhood
High revel hold aright, and mirthful was their
mood:
Oft-times on tourney bent those gallants sought
the field,
And gentle knights in joust would shiver spear
and shield;
Anon would seek the court for sport and carol
gay-
For fifteen days full told the feast was held
alway,
With all the meat and mirth that men might well
devise,
Right glorious was the glee that rang in riotous
wise.
Glad clamour through the day, dancing
throughout the night;
Good luck throughout the hall and chambers
well bedight,
Had lords and ladies fair, each one as pleased
him best,
With all of this world's weal they dwelt, those
gallant guests;
For Christ no braver knights had faced or toil or
strife,
No fairer ladies e'er had drawn the breath of
life,

so I want to tell of an adventure that happened
in his time, which some men think is a miracle,
and is the strangest of the Arthurian stories.
If you will listen to my song for a while I
promise
I'll tell it to you as I heard it truthfully told in
town -
that is, a powerful story,
well set out,
sweetly written,
that the people have known a long time.

The King was at Camelot, and it was Christmas
time,
with many handsome lords, and also gallant
knights,
and the whole brotherhood of the round table
held great celebrations, and they were happy:
many times these brave men had fought in
tournaments,
and sweet knights would split their spears and
shields jousting;
then they would come back to the court for
pleasure and singing–
the feast was always celebrated for a whole
fifteen days,
with all the food and jollity that men can invent,
the jolly pleasure that rang through the halls
was glorious.
There was a happy noise throughout the day,
dancing throughout the night;
the greatest happiness throughout the hall and
the rooms
was enjoyed by the fair lords and ladies, each
one doing what they liked best,
they had all the world's happiness, those brave
guests;
no braver knights had ever faced labour or
battle for Christ,
no more beautiful ladies had ever lived,
and he, the most handsome king that ever ruled,
truly,
for all these good people were still young, and
still
the happiest on earth,

And he, the comeliest king that e'er held court, forsooth,
For all this goodly folk were e'en in their first youth,
and still,
The happiest under heaven,
A king of stalwart will,
'T were hard with them to even
Another host on hill!

with a good strong king,
nobody can name
another group to match them!

IV

So young the New Year was, methinks it just was born,
Double upon the dais they served the meat that morn;
Into the hall he came, with all his knights, the King,
E'en as the chapel choir to end the mass did sing.
Loud rang the voice of clerk and cantor there aloft,
"Nowell, Nowell!" they sang, and cried the word full oft.
And sithen forth they run for handsel fair and free
Their New Year's gifts they pray, or give them readily.
And then about the gifts they make debate enow,
And ladies laugh full loud, tho' they have lost, I trow!
And this I rede ye well, not wroth was he who won!-
And all this mirth they made till meal-time came-anon
The board was set, they washed, and then in order meet
The noblest aye above, each gallant took his seat.
When Gaynore, gayly clad, stepped forth among them all,
Upon the royal dais, high in the midmost hall.
Sendal swept at her side, and eke above her head
A tapestry of Tars, and choice Toulouse outspread,
And all embroidered fair, and set with gems so

The New Year was so young, it had only just arrived,
and they served a double helping of food on the table that morning;
the King came into the hall with all his knights, just as the chapel choir were singing to end the mass.
The voice of the clerk and choirmaster rang out loudly from on high,
"Noel, Noel!" they sang, and repeated the word often.
And then they brought out with their lovely generous hands
their New Year's gifts, offering them around.
There was great debate as to who would have which gift,
and the ladies laughed out loud, even when they lost!
And I can tell you, the man who won was not upset!
They kept on with this jollity until soon it was time to eat;
the table was set, they washed, and then in the proper order
everyone took their seats, with the most noble at the head.
Queen Guinevere, beautifully dressed, was seated amongst them,
on the royal platform, the highest place in the hall.
She had rich silk surrounding her, and also above her head
there were tapestries from Tars and rich materials from Toulouse,
all beautifully embroidered, and studded with such wonderful gems,

8

gay
That might be proved of price, an ye their worth would pay
one day;
Right fair she was, the queen,
With eyes of shining grey,
That fairer he had seen
No man might soothly say!

the best that could be bought;
truly beautiful this Queen was,
with shining grey eyes,
no man could truly say
he had ever seen better!

V

Arthur, he would not eat till all were served with food,
Glad of his gladness he, somewhat of child-like mood;
A changeful life he loved, he liked it not a whit,
Either o'er-long to lie, or e'en o'er-long to sit,
So chafed his youthful blood, and eke his busy brain.
Also a custom good, to which the King was fain-
Thro' valour 'stablished fast-that never would he eat
On such high holiday ere yet adventure meet
Were told unto his ear-or wondrous tale enow,
Or else some marvel great that he might well allow-
Tales of his father's days, of arms, of emprise high,-
Or e'en some knight besought another's skill to try,
To join with him in joust, in jeopardy to lay
Life against life, each one, on hap of knightly play.
As Fortune them might aid-in quest of honour fair-
This was his custom good when as in court he were
At each high holiday, among his courtiers there in hall,
Fair-faced, and free of fear,
He sitteth o'er them all,
Right keen in that New Year,
And maketh mirth withal.

Arthur would not eat until everyone had been served,
grateful for his happiness, and somewhat boyish in mood;
he loved the active life, he didn't like at all
to lie in too long, or even to sit for too long,
his young blood and busy brain urged him on so much.
There was also a good custom the King insisted on–
it was a point of honour that he would never eat
on such festival days before a story
of some great adventure was told to him,
or some great miracle which he could believe–
tales of his father's days, feats of arms, great endeavours–
or even how some knight tested the skill of another,
facing him in a joust, each one putting
their life in danger for the sake of a gallant game.
So as fortune would permit–looking for sweet honour–
this was his excellent custom when he sat in court
on each high holiday, among his courtiers in the hall,
fair faced and fearless,
he sits above them all,
youthful that New Year,
celebrating with everyone.

VI

Thus in his place he stands, the young and

So he stood in his place, the brave young king,

gallant king,
Before the royal board, talking of many a thing.
There good Gawain, gay clad, beside Gaynore
doth sit,
Agravain "dure main," beyond her as is fit;
(Both the King's sister's sons, and knights of
valiant mood-)
High at the table sits Baldwin the Bishop good,
And Ywain, Urien's son, doth with the Bishop
eat-
These on the dais are served, in seemly wise,
and meet.
Full many a gallant knight sits at the board
below;
See where the first course comes, while loud the
trumpets blow!
With many a banner bright that gaily waves
thereby,
And royal roll of drums, and pipes that shrill on
high.
Wild warblings waken there, and sweet notes
rise and fall,
Till many a heart swelled high within that castle
hall!
Dainties they bring therewith, and meats both
choice and rare-
Such plenty of fresh food, so many dishes bear,
They scarce might find a place to set, the folk
before,
The silver vessels all that savoury messes bore,
on cloth,
The guests they help themselves,
Thereto they be not loth,
Each twain had dishes twelve,
Good beer, and red wine both.

VII

Now of their service good I think no more to
say,
For each man well may wot no lack was there
that day.
Noise that to them was new methinks now drew
anear
Such as each man in hall were ever fain to hear,
For scarce the joyful sounds unto an end were
brought,

at the royal table, talking of many things.
Good Gawain, brightly dressed, sat beside
Guinevere,
with Agravain, "the hard hand," the other side
as was right;
(both sons of the king's sister, and very brave
knights)
in a high place was sitting the good Bishop
Baldwin,
and Ywain, son of Urien, ate with the Bishop–
those on the dais were served in the proper
order.
Many gallant knights sat at the table below;
then came the first course, with the trumpets
loudly blowing!
Many bright banners were waved gaily as it
came,
and there was a royal roll of drums and playing
of shrill pipes.
The music raced around, sweet notes rising and
falling,
until many hearts inside the castle hall were
uplifted!
delicacies were brought along, with fine and
rare meats–
so much fresh food, so many dishes,
they could hardly find a place to put them down
before the diners,
that silverware which carried various different
stews, on the cloth;
the guests helped themselves,
and they were very happy to,
there were twelve dishes between each pair,
and good beer and red wine too.

Now I think I will say no more about the service
they had,
everyone can well imagine there was no lack
there that day.
Now they heard a noise coming near they hadn't
heard before,
something quite new to every man in the hall,
for the happy music had hardly finished,
and the first course had hardly been properly

And scarce had the first course been fitly served at court,
When through the hall door rushed a champion, fierce and fell,
Highest in stature he, of all on earth who dwell!
From neck to waist so square, and eke so thickly set,
His loins and limbs alike, so long they were, and great,
Half giant upon earth, I hold him to have been,
In every way of men the tallest he, I ween-
The merriest in his might that e'er a joust might ride,
Sternly his body framed in back, and breast, and side,
Belly and waist alike were fitly formed, and small,
E'en so his features fair were sharply cut withal, and clean,
Men marvelled at his hue,
So was his semblance seen,
He fared as one on feud,
And overall was green!

VIII

All green bedight that knight, and green his garments fair
A narrow coat that clung straight to his side he ware,
A mantle plain above, lined on the inner side
With costly fur and fair, set on good cloth and wide,
So sleek, and bright in hue-therewith his hood was gay
Which from his head was doffed, and on his shoulders lay.
Full tightly drawn his hose, all of the self-same green,
Well clasped about his calf-there-under spurs full keen
Of gold on silken lace, all striped in fashion bright,
That dangled beneath his legs-so rode that gallant knight.
His vesture, verily, was green as grass doth grow,

served to the court,
when in through the hall door rushed a fighter, fierce and dangerous,
the tallest man of anyone on earth!
His torso was so square and so thick,
with legs and arms to match, so long and huge,
I believe he must have been half giant,
certainly larger than any other man, I'm sure–
and the jolliest who might ever have ridden in a joust,
with his great back, chest and sides, his belly and waist were nicely shaped, and small,
and his fair features were chiselled and clean;
men were amazed by his colour,
by what they saw in front of them,
he looked ready for a fight,
and all over he was green!

That knight was green all over, and his clothes were also green;
he wore a tight fitting coat that hung straight down his sides,
a plain cloak over it, lined on the inside with good expensive fur on good wide cloth,
so smooth and brightly coloured–his bright hood
was off his head and lying on his shoulders.
His stockings were close-fitting, of the same green colour,
hugging nicely round his calves; underneath he had sharp spurs
made of gold with silk straps, shining brightly,
that dangled under his legs–that was the style of that gallant knight.
His clothes were truly as green as the growing grass,
the metal bars on his belt and the jewels surrounding them,
generously spread out across his whole

The barring of his belt, the blithe stones set
arow,
That decked in richest wise his raiment fine and
fair,
Himself, his saddle-bow, in silken broideries
rare,
'T were hard to tell the half, so cunning was the
wise
In which 't was broidered all with birds, and eke
with flies!
Decked was the horse's neck, and decked the
crupper bold,
With gauds so gay of green, the centre set with
gold.
And every harness boss was all enamelled
green,
The stirrups where he stood were of the self
same sheen,
The saddle-bow behind, the girths so long and
fair,
They gleamed and glittered all with green stones
rich and rare,
The very steed beneath the self same semblance
ware,
he rides
A green horse great and tall;
A steed full stiff to guide,
In broidered bridle all
He worthily bestrides!

costume,
on himself, on his saddle, on silken embroidery,
it would be hard to describe half of it, it was so
skilful
the way it was embroidered over with birds and
also with butterflies!
The horse's neck was decorated, and so was his
crupper,
with ornaments of green studded with gold.
Every piece of the harness was painted green,
and the stirrups he was using were the same
colour,
the skirts of his saddle, the girths so long and
beautiful,
they gleamed and glittered with rare green
jewels,
and the horse itself was exactly the same colour,
he rode
a green horse huge and tall;
a difficult horse to ride,
dressed in an embroidered bridle,
a worthy mount for him!

IX

Right gaily was the knight bedecked, all green
his weed,
The hair upon his head, the mane of his good
steed,
Fair floating locks enfold his shoulders broad
and strong,
Great as a bush the beard that on his breast low
hung,
And, with his goodly hair that hung down from
his head,
A covering round his arms, above his elbows,
spread.
Laced were his arms below, e'en in the self-
same way
As a king's cap-a dos, that clasps his neck

That knight was dressed so gaily, with his
clothes all green,
and the hair on his head, the mane of his good
horse,
fair floating locks covering his broad strong
shoulders,
his beard hanging down his chest like a great
bush,
and the fine hair that hung down from his head
was cut round the level of his elbows, spread
so his arms were hidden beneath it, in the same
way
that the King's cloak fits tightly around his neck.
The mane of the great horse was very much the
same,

alway.
The mane of that great steed was well and deftly wrought,
Well crisped and combed the hair, with many a knot in-caught.
Folded with golden thread about the green so fair,
Here lay a twist of gold, and here a coil of hair.
In self-same wise the tail and top-most crest were twined,
A band of brightest green the twain alike did bind,
Which, set with precious stones, hung the tail's length adown,
Then, twisted in a knot, on high the crest did crown.
There-from hung many a bell, of burnished gold so bright.,
Such foal upon the fell, bestridden by such knight,
Sure ne'er within that hall before of mortal sight were seen,
As lightning gleaming bright
So seemed to all his sheen,
They deemed that no man might
Endure his blows so keen.

X

Nor helmet on his head, nor hauberk did he wear,
Gorget nor breast-plate good, as knights are wont to bear;
Nor shaft to smite, nor shield that blows might well withstand,
Naught but a holly bough he carried in one hand,
(When all the groves be bare then fullest is its green),
And in his other hand a huge axe, sharp and sheen,
A weapon ill to see, would one its fashion say,
The haft, it measured full an ell-yard long alway,
The blade of good green steel, and all with gold inlaid,
Right sharp and broad the edge, and burnished

well combed and curled, with ornamental knots tied in.
Golden thread was plaited in with the green,
so that here there was a strand of gold and here a twist of hair.
The tail and the top of his head were plaited in the same way,
and a bright green band held them both in place,
which, set with precious stones, hung down the length of the tail,
and then crowned his head with a twist did not.
Many golden bells hung from this band.
Such a living horse, ridden by such a knight,
had certainly never been seen by any man in that hall before;
he seemed to shine
like bright gleaming lightning,
and everyone thought nobody
could match him in a fight.

He had no helmet on his head, and wore no mail shirt,
neither did he have a breastplate like knights usually do;
he had no spear to attack, or shield for defence,
all he carried was holly branch in one hand,
(they are at their greenest when all the forests are bare)
and in the other hand he carried a huge axe, sharp and shiny,
a terrifying weapon, looking at it one could see the head was a good yard long,
the blade was made of good green steel, inlaid with gold,
with a sharp broad edge, and a brightly polished blade.
It was sharpened to cut like a good razor,
and the steel was set in a handle of stiff wood

bright the blade.
'T was sharpened well to cut, e'en as a razor good,
Right well the steel was set in staff so stiff of wood,
And iron bands to bind throughout the length it bare,
With cunning work of green all wrought, and graven fair.
Twined with a lace that fell in silken loops so soft
E'en at the head, adown the haft 't was caught full oft
With hanging tassells fair that silken threads entwine,
And buttons of bright green, all broidered fair and fine.
Thus in the great hall door the knight stood, fair and tall,
Fearless and free his gaze, he gat him down the hall,
Greeting he gave to none, but looked right steadily
Toward the royal seat, and quoth, "Now where is he,
The lord of all this folk? To see him am I fain,
And with himself would speak, might I the boon attain!"-
With frown
He looked upon the knights,
And paced him up and down,
Fain would he know aright
Who was of most renown!

XI

Then each man gazed amain, each would that hero see,
And each man marvelled much what might the meaning be,
That man and horse, alike, of such a hue were seen,
Green as the growing grass; and greener still, I ween,
E'en than enamel green on gold that gloweth bright:
Then all with one consent drew near unto that

with iron bands to hold it all the way down,
all fashioned in green and beautifully engraved.
It was wrapped round with lace that fell in soft silken loops
from the head all down the handle it was wrapped
with lovely hanging tassles plaited from silken thread,
hanging from bright green studs, beautifully embroidered.
So the knight stood in the great doorway of the hall, fair and tall,
looking around him fearlessly and openly he walked down the hall,
he acknowledged no one, but looked straight ahead
towards the royal throne, and said, "Now where is he,
the ruler of all these people? I want to see him,
and I want to speak to him, so I can ask for a favour!"
He looked at the knights with a frown and marched up and down,
for he demanded to know
who was the most famous!

Then every man stared at him, everyone watching the hero,
and every man wondered what this could all mean,
seeing the man and horse both of the same colour,
green as the growing grass; I think he was more green
than green enamel painted over glowing gold:
then with one thought they all came close to the knight,

14

knight,
A-marvelling fell they all who he might be, ywis,
For strange sights had they seen, but none so strange as this!
The folk, they deemed it well fantasm, or fa.rie,
And none among them all dare answer speedily,
But all, astonied, gazed, and held them still as stone,
Throughout that goodly hall, in silence every one,
Their faces changed, as they by sleep were overcome,
suddenly,
I deem not all for fear,
But some for courtesy,
They fain would lend an ear
And let the King reply.

XII

Arthur before his dais beheld this marvel fair,
And boldly did he speak for dread, he knew it ne'er-
And said: Right welcome, Sir, to this my house and hall,
Head of this hostel I, and Arthur, men me call.
Alight from this thy steed, and linger here, I pray,
And what thy will may be hereafter shalt thou say."
"So help me," quoth the knight, "the God who rules o'er all,
I came not here to bide within thy castle wall,
The praise of this thy folk throughout the world is told,
Thy burg, thy barons all, bravest and best they hold,
The stiffest under steel who battle-steed bestride,
Wisest and worthiest they, throughout the whole world wide,
Proven right well in joust, and all fair knightly play,
Renowned for courtesy-so have I heard men say-
And this hath brought me here, e'en at this

and they all started wondering who he could be, for they
had certainly seen some strange sights, but none as strange as this!
The people thought it must be a ghost, or spirit, and none of them dared to make an answer,
but everybody stood as still as stone, staring in astonishment,
all through that great hall everybody was silent,
and their faces suddenly changed as if sleep had overcome them,
I don't think they were all frightened,
some were quiet out of courtesy,
they didn't want to answer
before the king had spoken.

Arthur saw this astonishing sight in front of his dais,
and spoke out boldly, for he had never been afraid–
and said: "You are very welcome Sir, to my house and hall,
I am the head of this residence, and people call me Arthur.
Get down from your horse and stay here, I pray, and then you can let us know what you want."
"I swear," said the knight, "by the God who rules over everything,
I haven't come here to live inside your castle, your people are praised throughout the world,
your castle and all your men are thought to be the bravest and the best,
the strongest who ever put on armour and climbed on a warhorse,
the wisest and best throughout the whole world, who have proved themselves in jousting and all knightly games,
famous for courtesy–that's what I've heard men say–
and this brought me here, even at Christmas time,
for you can be assured by this green branch I

Yule-tide fair,
For be ye well assured by this green branch I bear
That I would pass in peace, and seek no battle here-
For an it were my will to ride in warlike gear
I have at home an helm, and hauberk good and strong,
A shield and shining spear, with blade both sharp and long,
And other weapons good, that well a knight beseem,
But since I seek no war my weeds are soft, I ween,
And if ye be so bold as all men say ye be
The favour that I ask ye sure will grant to me of right,"
Arthur, he was not slow
To speak, "I trow, Sir Knight,
An here thou seek'st a foe
Thou shalt not fail for fight!"

XIII

"Nay, here I crave no fight, in sooth I say to thee,
The knights about thy board but beardless bairns they be,
An I were fitly armed, upon this steed so tall,
For lack of strength no man might match me in this hall!
Therefore within thy court I crave a Christmas jest,
'T is Yuletide, and New Year, and here be many a guest,
If any in this hall himself so hardy hold,
So valiant of his hand, of blood and brain so bold,
That stroke for counter-stroke with me exchange he dare,
I give him of free gift this gisarme rich and fair,
This axe of goodly weight, to wield as he see fit,
And I will bide his blow, as bare as here I sit.
If one will test my words, and be of valiant mood,
Then let him swiftly come, and take this weapon good,-

am carrying
that I have come in peace, and I'm not looking for battle–
because if I wanted to ride in armour
I have a helmet at home, and good chainmail,
a shield and a shining spear, with a sharp long blade,
and other good weapons suitable for a knight,
but since I am not seeking battle my clothes are soft,
and if you are as brave as everyone says you are
you will certainly grant me the favour I ask you."

Arthur was not slow
to speak, "I believe, Sir Knight,
that if you are looking for an opponent,
you won't be lacking in them!"

"No, I don't want to fight, I'm telling you in truth,
the knights around your table are only beardless babies,
and if I were properly armed, on my great horse,
no man in this hall would be strong enough to fight me!
So I'm looking for a Christmas game in your court,
it is Christmas, and New Year, and you have many guests here,
if anyone in this hall thinks he is strong enough,
with such strong hands, so brave in blood and brain,
that he dares to exchange blow for blow with me,
I will give him a free gift of this splendid axe,
a good heavy weapon, to use as he thinks fit,
and I will endure his blow, undefended as I am.
If anyone wants to put me to the test, and is brave enough,
then let him step forward, and take this good

Here I renounce my claim, the axe shall be his own-
And I will stand his stroke, here, on this floor of stone,
That I in turn a blow may deal, that boon alone I pray,
Yet respite shall he have
A twelvemonth, and a day.
Now quickly I thee crave-
Who now hath aught to say?"

XIV

If erst they were amazed, now stiller sat they all,
Both high and low, those knights within King Arthur's hall,
The knight upon his steed he sat him fast and true,
And round about the hall his fierce red eyes he threw,
From 'neath his bushy brows, (all green they were in hue,)
Twisting his beard he waits to see if none will rise,
When no man proffers speech with mocking voice he cries,
"What, is this Arthur's house? Is this his gallant band
Whose fame hath run abroad through many a realm and land?
Where be your vaunted pride? Your conquests, where be they?
Your wrath, and fierceness fell, your boastful words alway?
Now is the Table Round, its revel and renown,
O'erthrown with but a word from one man's mouth alone,
Since none dare speak for dread tho' ne'er a dint he see.-"
With that he laughed so loud Arthur must sham.d be,
And in his face so fair the blood rose ruddily alight,
As wind waxed wroth the King
And every gallant knight,
In words of warlike ring
He hailed that man of might.

weapon-
I give up my claim to it, the axe shall be his-
and I will face his blow, here, on the stone floor,
all I ask is that I can give a blow of my own,
but he shall not receive it
for a year and a day.
Now I ask you, if anyone will answer,
let him do it quickly!"

If they were astonished before, now they were even more so,
the highest and the lowest, those knights inside King Arthur's Hall,
the knight sat on his horse solid and steadfast,
staring round the hall with his fierce red eyes
from underneath his bushy brows (they were all green in colour)
twisting his beard and waiting to see if anyone came forward,
and when nobody said anything he cried out in a mocking voice,
"What, is this the house of Arthur? Is this his brave band
who are famous throughout the world?
Where is your great pride? Where are your triumphs?
Your anger, your terrible fierceness, your boastful words?
Now the whole of the round table, its joy and fame,
is overthrown by just a word from one man's mouth,
you are all terrified even though no blow has been offered!"
At that he laughed so loudly that Arthur was ashamed,
and the blood rushed into his face,
he became as angry as a storm,
and so did every brave knight,
and speaking with a warlike voice
he addressed that mighty man.

XV

And quoth, "By Heaven, Sir Knight, thou speakest foolishly,
But what thy folly craves we needs must grant to thee,
I trow no knight of mine thy boastful words doth fear,
That goodly axe of thine in God's name give me here,
And I will give the boon which thou dost here demand!"
With that he lightly leapt, and caught him by the hand,
Then lighted down the knight, before the King he stood,
And Arthur, by the haft he gripped that axe so good,
And swung it sternly round, as one who thought to smite;
Before him on the floor he stood, that stranger knight,
Taller by full a head than any in the hall,
With stern mien did he stand, and stroked his beard withal,
And drew his coat adown, e'en with unruffled cheer,
No more was he dismayed for threats he needs must hear
Than at the royal board one bare a cup anear of wine,
Gawain from out his place
Spake fitting words and fine,
" I pray thee of thy grace
Be this adventure mine!"

XVI

Quoth Gawain to the King, "I pray right worthily
Thou bid me quit this seat, and take my stand by thee,
That so without reproach, I from this board may rise,
And that it be not ill in my liege lady's eyes,
I'll to thy counsel come before this royal court,
Unfitting do I deem that such a boon be sought,
And such a challenge raised in this your goodly

And said, "By heaven, Sir Knight, you are speaking foolishly,
but we must give you what your foolishness demands,
I believe no knight of mine would be afraid of your boastful words,
in the name of God give me that good axe of yours,
and I will give you the favour you're asking for!"
With that he skipped forward and caught him by the hand,
and the knight dismounted and stood before the King,
and Arthur gripped the shaft of the excellent axe,
and swung it sternly around, like someone who was about to give a blow;
that strange knight stood on the floor in front of him,
taller by a head than anyone else in the hall,
he stood with a stern face, stroking his beard,
and drew back his coat, undisturbed,
no more upset by the threats he was offered
then if somebody had offered him a glass of wine.
From his place Gawain
spoke good and proper words,
"I pray you by your Grace
let me have this adventure!"

Gawain said to the King, "I beg you
to ask me to leave my seat and stand by you,
so that I can leave this table without criticism,
and if it does not seem wrong to my Queen,
I'll give you advice in front of this royal court;
I think it's wrong for him to ask for this favour,
and to give such a challenge in your great hall,
and for you to have to answer it,
while there are many brave knights sitting beside you—

hall
That thou thyself be fain to answer it withal,
While many a valiant knight doth sit beside thee
still-
I wot there be 'neath Heaven no men of sterner
will,
Nor braver on the field where men fight as is fit-
Methinks, the weakest I, the feeblest here of wit,
The less loss of my life, if thou the sooth
would'st say!
Save as thy near of kin no praise were mine
alway,
No virtue save thy blood I in my body know!
Since this be folly all, nor thine to strike this
blow,
And I have prayed the boon, then grant it unto
me,
This good court, an I bear myself ungallantly,
may blame!"
Together did they press,
Their counsel was the same,
To free the King, no less,
And give Gawain the game.

XVII

Then did the King command that gallant knight
to rise,
And swiftly up he gat in fair and courteous wise,
And knelt before his lord, and gripped the axe's
haft,
The King, he loosed his hold, and raised his
hand aloft,
And blessed him in Christ's Name, and bade
him in good part
To be of courage still, hardy of hand and heart.
"Now, Nephew, keep thee well," he quoth, "deal
but one blow,
And if thou red'st him well, in very truth I know
The blow that he shall deal thou shalt right well
withstand!"
Gawain strode to the knight, the gisarme in his
hand,
Right boldly did he bide, no whit abashed, I
ween,
And frankly to Gawain he quoth, that knight in
green,

I swear that there are no men on earth braver,
no better on the battlefield where men fight
properly–
I know that I am the weakest and most foolish,
and would be the smallest loss, to tell the truth!
I've never been praised except as your kinsman,
and I have no virtues apart from the blood of
yours I have in my body!
This business is foolishness, you shouldn't have
to strike,
and I have asked for the favour, so give it to me,
if I behave ungallantly this good court can
blame me!"
They all gathered round,
all with the same advice,
that the king should hand over
his place to Gawain.

Then the king ordered that brave knight to rise,
and he swiftly got up in courteous fashion,
and knelt in front of his Lord, and took the shaft
of the axe;
the King loosened his grip and lifted up his
hand,
and blessed him in the name of Christ, and told
him
to be brave, strong in heart and body.
"Now, nephew, be careful," he said, "to give
just one blow,
and if you do it right then I am certain
as you will also survive the blow he gives you!"
Gawain strode up to the knight, the axe in his
hand;
he waited for him boldly, not at all embarrassed,
and the Green Knight spoke frankly to Gawain;
"Let us make an agreement here, before we go
any further;
the first thing I ask, Sir Knight, is to know your
name;

"Make we a covenant here, ere yet we further
go,
And first I ask, Sir Knight, that I thy name may
know,
I bid thee tell me true, that I assured may be-"
"I' faith," quoth that good knight, "Gawain, I
wot, is he
Who giveth thee this blow, be it for good or ill,
A twelvemonth hence I'll take another at thy
will,
The weapon be thy choice, I'll crave no other
still
alive!"
The other quoth again,
"Gawain, so may I thrive,
But I shall take full fain,
The dint that thou shalt drive!"

XVIII

"By Christ," quoth the Green Knight, "I trow I
am full fain
The blow that here I craved to take from thee,
Gawain,
And thou hast well rehearsed, in fashion fair, I
trow,
The covenant and the boon I prayed the king but
now;
Save that thou here, Sir Knight, shalt soothly
swear to me
To seek me out thyself, where e'er it seemeth
thee
I may be found on field, and there in turn
demand
Such dole as thou shalt deal before this goodly
band!"
"Now," quoth the good Gawain, "by Him who
fashioned me,
I wot not where to seek, nor where thy home
shall be,
I know thee not, Sir Knight, thy court, nor yet
thy name,
Teach me thereof the truth, and tell me of that
same,
And I will use my wit to win me to that goal,
And here I give thee troth, and swear it on my
soul!"

I order you to tell me the truth, so I can be sure–
"
*"By God," said that good knight, "Gawain is
the*
*one who will give you this blow, whether it's
good or bad,*
*and a year from now I shall take another one
from you;*
*you can choose your weapon, but I'll face no
one but you!"*
The other spoke again,
"Gawain, I swear,
I'm very glad that it's you
who will be giving me the blow!"

*"By Christ," said the Green Knight, "I say I am
most satisfied*
*that I will take the blow I asked for from you,
Gawain,*
and you have done exactly the right things,
*to make the promise and give the favour I asked
from the King just now;*
*the other thing I ask, Sir Knight, is that you
swear to me*
*that you will look for me yourself, wherever you
think*
*I can be found, and when you find me that you
ask*
*for same gift that you will give in front of this
good company!"*
*"Now," said the good Gawain, "by the one who
made me,*
*I don't know where to look for you, or where
your home is,*
*I don't know you Sir Knight, your court, or your
name;*
tell me the answers to those questions
and I will use my intelligence to find you;
*I give you my promise, and I swear it on my
soul!"*
*"No, on this New Year that's all that's needed, I
think,"*

20

"Nay, in this New Year's tide it needs no more, I ween,"
So to the good Gawain he quoth, that knight in green,
"Save that I tell thee true-when I the blow have ta'en,
Which thou shalt smartly smite-and teach thee here amain
Where be my house, my home, and what my name shall be;
Then may'st thou find thy road, and keep thy pledge with me.
But if I waste no speech, thou shalt the better speed,
And in thy land may'st dwell, nor further seek at need
for fight
Take thy grim tool to thee,
Let see how thou can'st smite!"
Quoth Gawain, "Willingly,"
And stroked his axe so bright.

XIX

The Green Knight on the ground made ready speedily,
He bent his head adown, that so his neck were free,
His long and lovely locks, across the crown they fell,
His bare neck to the nape all men might see right well
Gawain, he gripped his axe, and swung it up on high,
The left foot on the ground he setteth steadily
Upon the neck so bare he let the blade alight,
The sharp edge of the axe the bones asunder smite-
Sheer thro' the flesh it smote, the neck was cleft in two,
The brown steel on the ground it bit, so strong the blow,
The fair head from the neck fell even to the ground,
Spurned by the horse's hoof, e'en as it rolled around,
The red blood spurted forth, and stained the

said the Green Knight to Gawain,
"Except that I'm telling you the truth–when I have taken the blow,
which you will give me–I shall tell you at once where is my house, my home, and what my name is;
then you can find your way there and keep your promise.
But if I do not talk, that will be better for you, and you can stay in your own country, not looking for a fight;
take up that terrible weapon,
and let's see how you can strike!
Gawain said, "Gladly,"
and stroked his bright axe.

The Green Knight made himself quickly ready on the ground,
he bent his head down, so that his neck was bare,
his long lovely hair fell forward from his head, all men could see the length of his bare neck.
Gawain gripped his axe and lifted it up high, putting his left foot firmly forward on the ground he let the blade fall upon the bare neck;
the sharp edge of the axe smashed the bones apart–
it went straight through the flesh, the neck was cut in two,
the blow was so strong that the brown steel bit into the ground,
and the handsome head came off the neck and rolled on the floor,
kicked by the horse's hoof even as it rolled around,
the red blood spurted out and stained all the bright green,
but that unknown knight never stumbled or fell; he quickly got up, on strong and firm legs, and reached out his hand, as everyone stared at

green so bright,
But ne'er for that he failed, nor fell, that stranger knight,
Swiftly he started up, on stiff and steady limb,
And stretching forth his hand, as all men gaped at him,
Grasped at his goodly head, and lift it up again,
Then turned him to his steed, and caught the bridle rein,
Set foot in stirrup-iron, bestrode the saddle fair,
The while he gripped his head e'en by the flowing hair.
He set himself as firm in saddle, so I ween,
As naught had ailed him there, tho' headless he was seen
in hall;
He turned his steed about,
That corpse, that bled withal,
Full many there had doubt
Of how the pledge might fall!

XX

The head, within his hand he held it up a space,
Toward the royal dais, forsooth, he turned the face,
The eyelids straight were raised, and looked with glance so clear,
Aloud it spake, the mouth, e'en as ye now may hear;
"Look, Gawain, thou be swift to speed as thou hast said,
And seek, in all good faith, until thy search be sped,
E'en as thou here didst swear, in hearing of these knights-
To the Green Chapel come, I charge thee now aright,
The blow thou hast deserved, such as was dealt to-day,
E'en on the New Year's morn I pledge me to repay,
Full many know my name, Ô Knight of the Chapel Green,'
To find me, should'st thou seek, thou wilt not fail, I ween,
Therefore thou need'st must come, or be for

him,
grasped his good head and lifted it up again,
then he turned to his horse, and caught hold of the bridle,
put his foot in the stirrup, and swung into the saddle.
All this time he was holding his head by its flowing hair.
He sat as firmly in the saddle as if
nothing had touched him, although he now had no head;
he turned his horse around,
that bleeding corpse,
and many were afraid
of how the business would end!

He held the head in his hand for a moment,
and then he turned the face towards the royal dais;
the eyelids opened, and it looked ahead clearly,
and it spoke aloud from the mouth, as you may now hear;
"Make sure, Gawain, you do what you have said,
and search faithfully until you have found your object,
just as you swore in the presence of these knights.
Come to the Green Chapel, I now order you;
I promise I will give you back the blow you deserve,
like the one you gave me today, on New Year's morning.
Many know my name, 'Knight of the Green Chapel,'
if you look for me you can't fail to find me,
and so you must come, or be called a coward!"
With a fierce pull on the reins he turned his horse around,
holding his head in his hand, and rode out of the hall,
with sparks flying from the hooves of his horse;

recreant found!"
With fierce pull at the rein he turned his steed around,
His head within his hand, forth from the hall he rode,
Beneath his horse's hoofs the sparks they flew abroad,
No man in all the hall wist where he took his way,
Nor whence that knight had come durst any of them say,
what then?
The King and Gawain there
They gazed, and laughed again,
Proven it was full fair
A marvel unto men!

XXI

Tho' Arthur in his heart might marvel much, I ween,
No semblance in his speech of fear or dread was seen
Unto the Queen he quoth, in courteous wise, and gay,
"Dear lady, at this tide let naught your heart dismay,
Such craft doth well, methinks, to Christmas-time belong,
When jests be soothly sought, with laugh and merry song,
And when in carols gay our knights and ladies vie-
Natheless unto my meat I'll get me presently,
I may not soon forget the sight mine eyes have seen!"
He turned him to Gawain, and quoth with gladsome mien,
"Now, Sir, hang up thine axe, the blow was soundly sped!"
'T was hung above the dais, on dossel overhead,
That all within the hall might look upon it well,
And by that token true the tale of wonder tell,
Then to the royal board they sat them down, those twain,
The King, and the good knight, and men for service fain

no man in the hall knew where he was going,
and none of them could say where the knight
had come from;
the King and Gawain
looked at him and laughed,
and everybody thought
it was a miracle!

Though I think Arthur was astonished in his heart,
in his speech no fear or dread could be seen.
He spoke to the Queen, courteously and merrily,
"Dear lady, don't let anything upset you at this time,
these tricks, I think, are very good at Christmas,
that's where they belong, when jokes are made
with laughter and merry songs,
when our knights and ladies compete with their carol singing–
although I will start my meal now,
I won't quickly forget what I've just seen!"
He turned to Gawain, and said with a smile,
"Now, sir, hang up your axe, you struck a good blow!"
It was hung up above the dais, on the tapestry,
so that everyone in the hall could see it,
and know that the story was true.
Then those two sat back down at the royal table,
the King and the good knight, and the serving men quite rightly
gave them a double portion of everything, as noblemen should have.
They spent the Yuletide feast with food and song,
and spent the day happily until the night came over the land;
now be careful Gawain,

As to the noblest there with double portion
wend-
With meat and minstrelsy the Yule-tide feast
they spend,
With joy they pass the day till shades of night
descend
o'er land,
Now think thee well, Gawain,
And fail not to withstand
The venture thou wast fain
To take unto thine hand!

*and do not fail to follow
the adventure
that you chose for yourself!*

Book Two

I

Now this first venture fair, befell in the New Year
To Arthur, who such feats was ever fain to hear;
Altho' his words were few whenas at meat they met;
But now to task full stern their hand methinks be set.
Right gladly did Gawain begin these games in hall,
If heavy be the end, small wonder were withal:
A man hath merry mind when he hath drunk amain,
Speedy, the year hath sped and cometh not again;
Beginnings to their end do all unlike appear-
The Yuletide passed away; and eke the after year
Each season severally after the other sent;
When Christmas-tide was past then came the crabb.d Lent,
That, changing flesh for fish, doth simpler food provide;
The weather of the world with winter then doth chide,
The cold no longer clings, the clouds themselves uplift,
Shed swift the rain, and warm, the showers of springtide drift,
Fall fair upon the field, the flowers all unfold,
The grass, and e'en the groves all green ye may behold.
The birds begin to build, and greet, with joyful song,
Solace of summer sweet, that followeth ere long-
On bank
The blossoms fair they blow
In hedgerow rich and rank;
The birds sing loud and low
In woodland deep and dank.

II

After the summer-tide, with gentle winds and soft,
When zephyr on the sward and seeds doth

Now the story of this great adventure started at New Year
for Arthur, who loved to hear about such things;
although they had little to discuss when they sat down to eat
they now had a stiff task to think about.
Gawain was happy to take on this challenge in the hall,
but it will be no surprise if the end is sad:
men can be happy when they've had plenty to drink,
but the year passes quickly and doesn't come back;
the beginning isn't often like the end–
the Yuletide passed away; and through the rest of the year
one season followed another;
when Christmas had passed then came starving Lent,
when meat is changed for fish and simpler food;
the weather everywhere fights against winter,
the cold no longer is everywhere, the clouds disappear,
the rain falls quickly and the warm spring showers come in,
falling sweetly on the field, and the flowers bloom,
you can see the grass and the woods all green.
The birds begin to build their nests and greet
the sweet summer with happy songs, which follows before long–
the flowers grow sweetly on the bank
and thickly in the hedges with their scent;
the birds sing loud and low
in the deep dark woods.

After the summertime, with its soft gentle winds,
when the breezes brief over the grass and the seeds,

breathe full oft,
(Full gladsome is the growth waxing therefrom, I ween,
Whenas the dewdrops drip from off the leaves so green,
Beneath the blissful beams of the bright summer sun)-
Then nigheth harvest-tide, hardening the grain anon,
With warnings to wax ripe ere come the winter cold,
With drought he drives the dust before him on the wold,
From off the field it flies, in clouds it riseth high;
Winds of the welkin strive with the sun, wrathfully,
The leaves fall from the bough, and lie upon the ground,
And grey is now the grass that erst all green was found;
Ripens and rots the fruit that once was flower gay-
And thus the year doth turn to many a yesterday,
Winter be come again, as needeth not to say the sage;
Then, when Saint Michael's moon
Be come with winter's gage
Gawain bethinks him soon
Of his dread venture's wage.

(I think the plants which grow from that are delightful,
when the dewdrops drip off the leaves so green,
beneath the sweet beams of the bright summer sun)—
then comes the harvest, with the ripening grain,
warning us to gather in before the cold winter comes,
he brings the drought and makes all the land dusty,
it flies off the fields, rising in high clouds;
in the sky wild winds struggle with the sun,
the leaves fall from the trees, and lie on the ground,
and the grass that once was green is now grey;
the fruit that was once as lovely as flowers ripens and rots—
and so what was the future becomes the past,
winter comes again, you don't need a wise man to tell you that:
then the Michaelmas moon comes
as warning of approaching winter,
and Gawain began to think
of the dreadful quest he had chosen.

III

Yet till All-Hallows' Day with Arthur did he bide,
Then for his sake the king a fair feast did provide,
Rich was the revel there of the good Table Round,
There were both courteous knights and comely ladies found,
And many sorrowed sore all for that good knight's sake-
Yet none the less no sign of aught but mirth they make,
Tho' joyless all the jests they bandy at that same-

But he stayed with Arthur until Halloween,
and in his honour the King held a great feast,
and there was splendid merrymaking at the round table;
there were many good knights and sweet ladies there,
and many were very sad for the sake of that good knight,
but despite that they all pretended to be merry,
although the jokes they made were joyless.
After the meal he spoke sadly to his uncle about his journey, and said openly:
"Now, ruling Lord over my life, I must ask to leave.

With mourning after meat he to his uncle came,
And of his journey spake, and openly did say:
"Now, liege Lord of my life, your leave I fain
would pray,
Ye know how stands the case, thereof no more
I'll speak-
Since talk, it mendeth naught, 't were trifling
ease to seek;
I to the blow am bound, to-morrow must I fare
To seek the Knight in Green, God knoweth how,
or where."
The best knights in the burg together then they
ran,
Ywain and Erec there, with many another man,
Dodinel le Sauvage; the Duke of Clarence came,
Lancelot, Lionel, and Lucain, at that same,
Sir Boors, Sir Bedivere, (the twain were men of
might,)
With Mador de la Port, and many another
knight.
Courtiers in company nigh to the king they
drew,
For counselling that knight, much care at heart
they knew.
In dole so drear their tears in hall together blend
To think that good Gawain must on such errand
wend
Such dolefull dint endure, no more fair blows to
spend
and free-
The knight he made good cheer,
He quoth: "What boots it me?
For tho' his weird be drear
Each man that same must dree."

IV

He dwelt there all that day, at early dawn
besought
That men would bring his arms, and all were
straightway brought.
A carpet on the floor they stretch full fair and
tight,
Rich was the golden gear that on it glittered
bright.
The brave man stepped thereon, the steel he
handled fair,

*You know the position, so I won't say any more
about it–
talk will not help, it can't change anything;
I am bound to take the blow, tomorrow I must
go
to look for the Green Knight, God knows how,
or where."
The best knights in the castle then gathered
round,
Ywain and Erec, with many others,
Dodinel le Sauvage; the Duke of Clarence came,
Lancelot, Lionel and Lucain with him,
Sir Boors, Sir Bedevere (both mighty men)
with Mador de la Port, and many other knights.
These courtiers all gathered round the King,
to advise that knight, all very sad at heart.
Many cried secretly to think
that good Gawain had to go on such a mission,
to receive such a terrible blow when he had
none to give back;
the knight remained cheerful,
and said: "What does it matter?
Even if a man's fate is dark,
he can't do anything about it."*

*He stayed there all day, and early in the
morning ordered
for his men to bring his arms, and they were all
brought at once.
They laid out a fine carpet on the floor,
and the golden gear that was laid on it glittered
brightly.
The brave man stepped forward and handled the
weapons,
and they put a tunic of Tharsian silk on him,*

A doublet dear of Tars they did upon him there,
A cunning cap-a-dos, that fitted close and well,
All fairly lined throughout, as I have heard it tell.
They set the shoes of steel upon the hero's feet,
And wrapped the legs in greaves, of steel, as fit and meet.
The caps that 'longed thereto polished they were full clean,
And knit about the knee with knots of golden sheen.
Comely the cuisses were that closed him all about
With thongs all tightly tied around his thighs so stout.
And then a byrnie bright with burnished steel they bring,
Upon a stuff so fair woven with many a ring.
And now upon each arm they set the burnished brace
With elbow plates so good-the metal gloves they lace;
Thus all the goodly gear to shield him was in place
that tide-
Rich surcoat doth he wear,
And golden spurs of pride,
His sword is girt full fair
With silk, upon his side.

V

When he was fitly armed his harness rich they deem,
Nor loop nor latchet small but was with gold a-gleam;
Then, harnessed as he was, his Mass he heard straightway,
On the high altar there an offering meet did lay.
Then, coming to the king, and to the knights at court,
From lords and ladies fair lightly his leave besought.
They kissed the knight, his soul commending to Christ's care-
Ready was Gringalet, girt with a saddle fair,

with a hooded cape that fitted close and well,
beautifully lined all through, so I've heard.
They put steel boots on the hero's feet,
and covered his legs with fine steel armour.
The knee pieces were polished until they shone
and were fixed around the knee with golden ties.
The beautiful thigh armour was tied
tightly to his muscular thighs.
Then they brought a mail shirt, made of bright steel
with the rings fixed to fine material.
On each arm they put shining armour,
with fine elbow plates; they laced on the metal gloves;
so he had on all the best armour for his protection:
he wore a fine coat over it
and splendid golden spurs,
with his trusty sword hung
at his side on a silken cord.

When he was fully armed he looked splendid,
the smallest piece of gear was gleaming with gold;
then, dressed as he was, he heard Mass at once,
on the high altar where a suitable offering was placed.
Then he came to the King, and to the knights of the court,
and lightly said goodbye to the lords and ladies.
They kissed the knight, asking Christ to watch over him;
his horse Gringalet was ready, wearing a fine saddle;
it gleamed merrily, fringed with gold,
and it had been refurbished for the adventure.

29

Gaily it gleamed that day, with fringes all of gold,
For this adventure high new nails it bare for old.
The bridle barred about, with gold adorn'd well,
The harness of the neck, the skirts that proudly fell,
Crupper and coverture match with the saddle-bow,
On all the red gold nails were richly set a-row,
They glittered and they gleamed, e'en as the sun, I wis-
The knight, he takes his helm, and greets it with a kiss.
'T was hooped about with steel, and all full fitly lined,
He set it on his head, and hasped it close behind.
Over the visor, lo! a kerchief lieth light,
Broidered about and bound with goodly gems and bright,
On a broad silken braid-there many a bird is seen
The painted perroquet appeareth there between
Turtles and true-love knots, so thick entwin'd there,
As maids seven winters long had wrought with labour fair
in town;
Full dear the circlet's price
That lay around the crown,
Of diamonds its device
That were both bright and brown.

VI

The shield they shewed him then, of flaming gules so red,
There the Pentangle shines, in pure gold burnish'd.
On baldric bound, the shield, he to his neck makes tight,
Full well I ween, that sign became the comely knight;
And why unto that prince the badge doth well pertain,
Tarry thereby my tale, I yet to tell am fain.
(For Solomon as sign erst the Pentangle set
In tokening of truth, it bears that title yet.)

The bridle was richly decorated with gold,
so was the harness, the saddle skirts,
the cropper and the horse cloth all matched,
with splendid gold nails in rows on red cloth,
they glittered and gleamed just like the sun.
The knight took his helmet and kissed it.
It was ringed with steel and well lined;
he put it on his head and fixed it tightly behind.
Over the visor there was a fine silk band,
embroidered and studied with fine bright gems
on the wide silk cloth; there could be seen many birds,
with painted parrots flying amongst
flowers with turtle doves thickly entwined;
it had taken seamstresses seven long winters to
make it in the town;
there was a valuable diadem
circling round the crown,
composed of diamonds,
clear and dark.

Then they showed him his shield, of deep crimson red,
shining with a pentangle picked out in gold.
He fixed the shield round his neck on its strap,
and I'm sure that sign was suited to that good knight;
and I would like to tell you why that Prince
was very well deserving of such a badge, even if
it slows down my story.
(For Solomon invented the pentangle as a sign of truth,
and it still means that to this day)
The shape is made of five points,

For 't is in figure formed of full five points I ween,
Each line in other laced, no ending there is seen.
Each doth the other lock-in English land, I wot,
It beareth everywhere the name of "Endless Knot."
Therefore as fitting badge the knight this sign doth wear,
For faithful he in five, five-fold the gifts he bare,
Sir Gawain, good was he, pure as refin'd gold,
Void of all villainy, virtue did him enfold,
and grace-
So the Pentangle new
Hath on his shield a place,
As knight of heart most true,
Fairest of form and face.

VII

First was he faultless found in his five wits, I ween;
Nor failed his fingers five where'er he yet had been;
And all his earthly trust upon those five wounds lay
That Christ won on the Cross, e'en as the Creed doth say.
And wheresoever Fate to fiercest fight did bring,
Truly in thought he deemed, above all other thing,
That all his force, forsooth, from those five joys he drew
Which through her Holy Child, the Queen of Heaven knew;
And for this cause the knight, courteous and comely, bare
On one half of his shield her image painted fair,
That when he looked thereon his courage might not fail
The fifth five that I find did much this knight avail
Were Frankness, Fellowship, all other gifts above,
Cleanness and Courtesy, that ever did him move,
And Pity, passing all-I trow in this fair five
That knight was clothed and happed o'er all that

and all the lines are interlocking, you can't see a finish.
Each one is twined with the other--in England I know
everyone calls it the "Endless knot."
So it was a good badge for the knight to wear,
for he was good in five ways, and five times in each of those ways,
Sir Gawain was good, pure as refined gold,
empty of all evil, he was wrapped in goodness and grace;
so the new Pentangle
had a place on his shield,
for the knight with the truest heart,
and the loveliest body and face.

Firstly he was faultless in all his five senses, I believe;
and his five fingers had never done any wrong;
and he put his trust in those five wounds which Christ won on the cross, as the Bible says.
And wherever fate brought the greatest challenges
he remained faithful in his thoughts, above all else,
and drew all his strength from those five joys which the Queen of Heaven had in her holy Child;
for this reason this good and handsome knight carried her image painted on one side of his shield,
so that he could look on her image and be brave.
The five qualities that I think were strong in this knight
were frankness, friendship, greater than any other gift,
cleanliness and courtesy, which he always displayed,
and pity, greater than everything; I believe that this knight
had more of these qualities than anyone on earth.
And all of these fivefold gifts rested on that

be alive.
And all these gifts, fivefold, upon that knight were bound,
Each in the other linked, that none an end had found.
Fast fixed upon five points, I trow, that failed him ne'er,
Nor joined at any side, nor sundered anywhere.
Nor was there any point, so cunningly they blend,
Where they beginning make, or where they find an end.
Therefore, upon his shield, fair-shapen, doth that same
Sign, in fair red gold gleam, upon red gules aflame,
Which the Pentangle pure the folk do truly name with lore
Armed is Sir Gawain gay,
His lance aloft he bore,
And wished them all "Good-day,"
He deemed, for evermore.

knight,
each one linked to the other, so no end could be found.
I believe he had faith in those five points which never failed him,
not joined anywhere, never divided.
They blended together so seamlessly that there was no point
where they started or finished.
So, on his shield, beautifully drawn, there was the same
sign, gleaming in red and gold on a crimson background,
which people are right to call the Pentangle of purity;
Sir Gawain was happy with his armour,
and he lifted his lance on high,
and said goodbye to them all,
forever, as he thought.

VIII

Spurs to his steed he set, and sprang upon his way,
So that from out the stones the sparks they flew alway-
Seeing that seemly sight the hearts of all did sink,
Each soothly said to each that which they secret think,
Grieved for that comely knight-"By Christ, 't were pity great
If yon good knight be lost, who is of fair estate;
His peer on field to find, i' faith, it were not light,
'T were better to have wrought by wile, methinks, than might!
Such doughty knight a duke were worthier to have been,
A leader upon land, gladly we such had seen!-
Such lot were better far than he were brought to naught,
Hewn by an elfish man, for gage of prideful thought!

He spurred on his horse, and galloped away,
so that the sparks flew out of the stones;
seeing that wonderful sight everyone's heart sank,
and everybody shared their secret thoughts,
grieving for that sweet knight: "By Christ, it would be a great shame
if that good knight is lost, who is such a fine man;
it would not be easy to find his match in battle,
I think it would have been best for him to be more cautious!
Such a fine knight would have been better as a duke,
he would have made such a good leader for this land!
That would have been far better than him being destroyed,
chopped down by some spirit for his arrogance!
Did any king ever agree to such a strange request,
and risk a good knight for a Christmas game?"

Did ever any king obey such strange behest,
As risk a goodly knight upon a Christmas jest?"
Much water warm, I ween, welled from the eyes
of all,
Whenas that gallant knight gat him from
Arthur's hall
that day:
Nor here would he abide,
But swiftly went his way,
By toilsome paths did ride,
E'en as the book doth say.

IX

Now rides Gawain the good thro' Logres' realm,
I trow,
Forth doth he fare on quest that seemeth ill
enow;
Often, companionless, at night alone must lie,
The fare he liketh best he lacketh verily;
No fellow save his foal hath he by wood or
wold,
With none save God alone that knight may
converse hold;
Till that unto North Wales full nigh he needs
must draw,
The isles of Anglesey on his left hand he saw;
And fared across the ford and foreland at that
same,
Over 'gainst Holyhead, so that he further came
To Wirral's wilds, methinks, nor long therein
abode
Since few within that land, they love or man, or
God!
And ever as he fared he asked the folk, I ween,
If they had heard men tell tale of a Knight in
Green
In all that land about? Or of a Chapel Green?
And all men answered, "Nay," naught of that
knight they knew,
And none had seen with sight a man who bare
such hue
as green;
The knight took roads full strange,
And rugged paths between,
His mood full oft did change
Ere he his goal had seen.

*I know that many tears fell from everyone's eyes
when that gallant knight left Arthur's hall that
day;
he would not stay there,
but went quickly on his way,
riding the hard roads,
so the story says.*

*Now the good Gawain went riding through
Logres' territory,
following his desperate mission;
he often had to lie alone at night,
lacking his favourite foods;
he had no friend in field or wood apart from his
horse,
and he could only talk to God;
at last he reached North Wales
and saw the islands of Anglesey on his left hand;
he crossed at the ford and headlands
at Holyhead, so that he went further
into the wilds of the Wirral, and didn't stay there
long
as there are few people in that land who love
either man God!
As he journeyed he was always asking people
if they had ever heard of a Green Knight
in that land? Or a Green Chapel?
And all the men answered they had never heard
of
or seen any knight in green;
the knight took many strange roads,
and also rocky paths,
his mood changed many times
before he reached his goal.*

X

Full many a cliff he climbs within that country's range,
Far flying from his friends he rideth lone and strange;
At every ford and flood he passed upon his way
He found a foe before, of fashion grim alway.
So foul they were, and fell, that he of needs must fight-
So many a marvel there befell that gallant knight
That tedious 't were to tell the tithe thereof, I ween
Sometimes with worms he warred, or wolves his foes have been;
Anon with woodmen wild, who in the rocks do hide-
Of bulls, or bears, or boars, the onslaught doth he bide;
And giants, who drew anigh, from off the moorland height;
Doughty in durance he, and shielded by God's might
Else, doubtless, had he died, full oft had he been slain.
Yet war, it vexed him less than winter's bitter bane,
When the clear water cold from out the clouds was shed,
And froze ere yet it fell on fallow field and dead;
Then, more nights than enow, on naked rocks he lay,
And, half slain with the sleet, in harness slept alway.
While the cold spring that erst its waters clattering flung
From the cliff high o'erhead, in icicles now hung.
In peril thus, and pain, and many a piteous plight
Until the Yuletide Eve alone that gallant knight did fare;
Sir Gawain, at that tide,
To Mary made his prayer,
For fain he was to ride
Where he might shelter share.

He climbed many cliffs in the hills of that country,
far away from his friends, riding alone, a foreigner;
at every ford or stream he crossed on his journey
he always found some grim enemy.
They were so revolting and evil that he had to fight–
so many extraordinary things happened to that brave knight
it would be difficult to tell a tenth of them, I think.
Sometimes he fought with dragons, others with wolves;
sometimes with wild men of the woods, who hid in the rocks–
he had to fight off attacks from bulls and bears and boars;
also giants, who came to him from the heights of the moors;
he was strong and steadfast, and protected by God,
otherwise he would doubtless have died many deaths.
But fighting troubled him less than the harsh winter,
with clear water falling cold out of the clouds,
freezing before it fell on the bare dead fields;
then he had more than enough nights lying on bare rock,
and, half killed by the snow, he always slept in his armour.
The cold spring which had once thrown down its chattering waters
from the high cliff overhead was now hung with icicles.
And so in danger and pain, through many terrible trials
the gallant knight travelled alone until Christmas Eve;
Sir Gawain, at that time,
said a prayer to Mary,
asking her to show him
where he could find shelter.

XI

That morn beside a mount his road the knight doth keep,
Threading a forest wild, with ways both strange and deep;
High hills on either hand, and holts full thick below,
Where hoar oaks, hundredfold, do close together grow;
Hazel and hawthorn there, in tangled thicket clung,
Ragged and rough, the moss o'er all a covering flung.
And many birds unblithe, on boughs ye might behold,
Piping full piteously, for pain of bitter cold.
Gawain, on Gringalet, fares lonely thro' the glade,
Thro' many a miry marsh, at heart full sore afraid
That he no shelter find, that, as was fit and right
He serve betimes that Sire, who, on that selfsame night
Was of a Maiden born, our bale to cure, I trow-
Therefore he, sighing, said: "Lord Christ, I pray Thee now,
And Mary Mother mild, for her Son's sake so dear,
A haven I may find, Thy mass may fitly hear,
And matins at the morn-meekly I crave this boon,
And Paternoster pray, and Ave too, right soon, with Creed-"
Thus praying, did he ride,
Confessing his misdeed,
Crossing himself, he cried:
"Christ's Cross me better speed!"

XII

Scarce had he signed himself, I ween, of times but three,
When there within the wood a dwelling doth he see;
Above a laund, on lawe, shaded by many a bough,
About its moat there stand of stately trees enow.

That morning the knight journeyed along beside a mountain,
threading through wild forest, through strange and deep paths;
there were high hills on either side, and great woods below,
where hundreds of grey oaks grew thickly together;
there were hazel and hawthorn there, wrapped in tangled thickets,
ragged and rough, all covered over with moss.
There were many unhappy birds to be seen on branches,
singing pitifully out of pain at the bitter cold.
Gawain, on Gringalet, road alone through the wood,
through many bogs and marshes, very worried that he would not be able to find a place where he could
worship his Lord, who had been born on that same night of a virgin, to end our troubles—
so he said, sighing, "Lord Christ, I pray to you now,
and to sweet mother Mary, for the sake of her dear son,
that I can find shelter where I can hear your mass properly,
and matins in the morning; I humbly ask this favour,
and I recite my Paternoster, my Ave Maria and creed."
So, praying, he rode on,
confessing to his sins,
he crossed himself and cried:
"May the cross of Christ help me!"

He had hardly crossed himself three times when he saw a dwelling within the wood;
it was on a knoll above the glade, shaded by many branches,
with plenty of great trees standing around its moat.
It was certainly a good castle for a fine strong

The comeliest castle sure, for owner strong and stout,
Set in a meadow fair with park all round about,
Within a palisade of spikes set thick and close,
For more than two miles round the trees they fast enclose;
Sir Gawain, from the side of that burg was aware,
Shimmered the walls, and shone, thro' oaken branches bare.
Then swift he doffed his helm, thanking, I trow, that day
Christ, and Saint Julian, that they had heard alway
Courteous, his piteous prayer, and hearkened to his cry-
"Now grant me," quoth the knight, "here right good hostelry."
Then pricked he Gringalet, with spurs of golden sheen,
The good steed chooseth well the chiefest gate, I ween.
And swift to the bridge end, he comes, the knight so keen,
at last;
The bridge aloft was stayed,
The gates were shut full fast,
The walls were well arrayed,
They feared no tempest's blast.

owner,
set in a lovely meadow with parks all around,
inside a fence of thick close spikes,
that enclosed the woods for more than two miles around;
from his side of the moat Sir Gawain gazed at the
shimmering walls which shone through the bare branches of the oaks.
Then he quickly took off his helmet, giving thanks
to Christ and St Julian, that they had been so good
to listen to his pitiful prayer and heard his request—
"Now give me," said the knight, "good shelter here."
So he urged on Gringalet with his golden spurs,
and the good horse chose the main gate.
He quickly came to the end of the bridge, that good knight;
the drawbridge was up,
the gates were bolted tight,
the walls were well built,
they feared no storm.

XIII

The knight upon the bank his charger there doth stay,
Beyond the double ditch that round the castle lay,
The walls, in water set they were, and wondrous deep,
And high above his head it towered, the castle keep;
Of hard stone, fitly hewn, up to the corbels fair,
Beneath the battlements the stones well shapen were.
Above 't was fairly set with turrets in between,
And many a loop-hole fair for watchman's gaze so keen.
A better barbican had never met his eye-

The knight stopped his charger upon the bank,
outside the double moat which ran round the castle;
the walls were set in water, and very deep,
and the tower of the castle stretched high above him;
it was made of hard stone, well shaped, up to the parapet,
beneath the battlements of the stones were well cut.
Above it there was a barbican, as good as he'd ever seen,
covered with turrets and with
many good loopholes for the watchmen to look through.

Within, the knight beheld a goodly hall and high,
The towers set between the bristling battlements,
Round were they, shapen fair, of goodly ornament,
With carven capitals, by cunning craft well wrought,
Of chalk-white chimneys too, enow they were he thought.
On battled roof, arow, they shone, and glittered white,
And many a pinnacle adorned that palace bright.
The castle cornices they crown'd everywhere
So white and thick, it seemed they pared from paper were.
Gawain on Gringalet right good the castle thought
So he might find within the shelter that he sought,
And there, until the feast to fitting end were brought
might rest,
He called, a porter came,
With fair speech, of the guest
He craved from wall his name,
And what were his behest?

XIV

"Good Sir," then quoth Gawain, "do thou for me this task,
Get thee unto thy lord, and say I shelter ask."
"Nay, by Saint Peter good," the porter quoth, "'t is well
Welcome be ye, Sir Knight, within these walls to dwell
Long as it liketh ye." Then swift his way he went,
As swiftly came again, with folk on welcome bent.
The drawbridge let adown, from out the gate they came,
And on the ground so cold they knelt low at that same,
To welcome that good knight in worthy wise that tide;

Inside, the knight could see a good high hall,
with towers set between the bristling battlements,
round, well shaped, nicely decorated,
with carved columns, well-made,
and with many chalk white chimneys.
They shone on the fortified roof, glittering white,
and many spires decorated that bright palace.
The mouldings on the castle covered everywhere,
so white and thick, it seemed they were cut from paper.
Gawain, sitting on Gringalet, thought it a fine castle,
and so that he could find the shelter he wished for inside
and rest there until the feast had come to its proper end,
he called, a porter came,
and speaking politely he asked
the name of the guest,
and what he wanted.

"Good sir," said Gawain, "do this thing for me,
go to your lord, and tell him I'm asking for shelter."
"No, by good Saint Peter," the porter said, "you are
very welcome, Sir Knight, to stay here
as long as you like." Then he swiftly disappeared,
and just as quickly came back, with welcoming folk.
The drawbridge was lowered and they came out the gate,
and they knelt down on the cold ground
to welcome that good knight properly at Christmas;
they led him to the gate with the doors wide open,

They shew to him the gate with portals opened wide,
Then o'er the bridge he gat, with greeting gay, the knight,
Serjants his stirrups seize, and bid him swift alight.
To stable that good steed the men run readily,
The knights and squires, they come adown full speedily,
To bring that gentle knight with bliss unto the hall
Whenas he raised his helm they hasted one and all,
To take it from his hand, to serve him are they fain,
His goodly sword and shield, in charge they take the twain.
Then greeting good he gave those nobles, every one,
The proud men, pressing nigh, to him have honour done,
Still in his harness happed, to hall they lead him there,
Upon the floor there flamed a fire both fierce and fair,
The castle's lord doth come forth from his chamber door,
To greet, with fitting grace, his guest upon the floor.
He quoth: "Be welcome here to stay as likes ye still,
For here all is your own to have at your own will,
and hold-"
"Gramercy," quoth Gawain,
"Of Christ be payment told,"
In courteous wise the twain
Embrace as heroes bold.

XV

Gawain gazed on the knight, who goodly greeting gave,
And deemed that burg so bright was owned of baron brave,
For huge was he in height, and manhood's age he knew,

then the knight rode over the bridge, with happy greetings,
and grooms grasped his stirrups, and told him to dismount.
The men took the good horse quickly to the stables,
and the knights and squires came down quickly to bring that sweet knight happily into the hall,
and when he took off his helmet they all hurried to take it from him, they all wanted to serve him,
and they relieved him of his sword and shield.
He gave each of these noblemen a warm greeting,
and these proud men gathered round to welcome him,
and they led him to the hall, still in his armour, where a good fire roared on the hearth.
The lord of the castle came out from his room, to welcome his guest properly in the hall.
He said, "You are welcome to stay here as long as you like, and you must treat this house as if it were your own-"
"I thank you," said Gawain,
"and Christ will reward you."
The two courteously
embraced as brave heroes do.

Gawain gazed at the knight who gave him this warm welcome,
and thought that the castle was owned by a great lord,
for he was very tall and a full grown man,
with a great beard on his chest, chestnut in

His broad beard on his breast, as beaver was its hue.
And stalwart in his stride, and strong, and straight, was he,
His face was red as fire, and frank his speech and free.
In sooth, Sir Gawain thought, 't would 'seem him well on land
To lead in lordship good of men a gallant band.
The lord, he led the way unto a chamber there,
And did his folk command to serve him fit and fair,
Then at his bidding came full many a gallant knight
They led him to a bower, with noble bedding dight.
The curtains all of silk, and hemmed with golden thread,
And comely coverings of fairest cloth o'er spread.
Above, of silk so bright, the broideries they were,
The curtains ran on ropes, with rings of red gold fair.
Rich tapestries of Tars, and Toulouse, on the wall
Hung fair, the floor was spread with the like cloth withal.
And there did they disarm, with many a mirthful rede,
The knight of byrnie bright, and of his warlike weed.
Then rich robes in their stead, I trow, they swiftly brought,
And for the change they chose the choicest to their thought.
Then soon he did them on, and I would have ye know,
Right well became the knight those skirts of seemly flow.
That hero, fair of face, he seem'd verily,
To all men who his mien and hue might nearer see
So sweet and lovesome there, of limb so light, they thought
That never Christ on earth a comelier had

colour.
He walked strong and straight, and his face was as red as fire, and he spoke freely and frankly.
Sir Gawain thought that he would be well suited as the leader of a band of gallant men.
The lord led the way to a room there and told his people to serve Gawain well, and at his orders many gallant knights came, and led him to an alcove, decked with fine bedding.
The curtains were all silk, hemmed with gold thread, and fine coverings of the best cloth were spread over all.
Above the canopies were of bright silk, embroidered, and the curtains ran on ropes, with rings of fine red gold.
Rich tapestries from Tars and Tolouse hung on the wall and the floor was covered with the same cloth.
There they took off his armour, with many happy jokes, relieving him of his bright coat and soldier's kit.
They quickly brought rich robes as a replacement, offering him the ones they thought were their best.
He quickly put them on and I can tell you that those fine clothes suited that knight very well.
To everyone who could see his face and colour, so fine and handsome, so light on his feet, they thought that Christ had never made a better man.
That knight, throughout the world, could certainly be said to be a prince without a peer on any battlefield.

wrought-
That knight
Thro' the world far and near
Might well be deemed of right
A prince with ne'er a peer
In field of fiercest fight.

XVI

A chair before the fire of charcoal, burning bright,
They set for good Gawain, with cloth all draped and dight.
Cushion and footstool fit, the twain they were right good,
Then men a mantle cast around him as he stood,
'T was of a bliaunt brown, broidered in rich device,
And fairly furred within with pelts of goodly price,
Of whitest ermine all, and even so the hood.
Down in that seemly seat he sat, the gallant good,
And warmed him at the fire-then bettered was his cheer;
On trestles fairly set they fix a table near
And spread it with a cloth, that shewed all clean and white,
Napkin and salt-cellar with silver spoons so bright.
The knight washed at his will, and set him down to eat,
Serjants, they served him there in seemly wise and meet;
With diverse dishes sweet, and seasoned of the best,
A double portion then they set before the guest,
Of fishes, baked in bread, or broiled on glowing wood,
Anon came fishes seethed, or stewed with spices good,
With choicest dainties there, as pleasing to his taste-
The knight, he quoth full oft, a feast that board had graced,
Then all, as with one voice, this answer made in haste:

*They set a chair before a bright charcoal fire
for good Gawain, covered in fine cloth.
There was a splendid cushion and footstool as well,
and men threw a cloak around him as he stood;
it was of spotless brown, embroidered with rich designs,
and lined with valuable furs of
the whitest ermine, even the hood.
He sat down in that pleasant seat, the brave good man,
and warmed himself at the fire–then he was made even happier;
on trestles nearby they fixed a tabletop
and spread a tablecloth across, all clean and white,
with napkins and salt cellars, and bright silver spoons.
The knight washed himself and sat down to eat.
Servants came to serve him respectfully and kindly;
they gave him many sweet dishes, beautifully seasoned,
and they gave the guest a double portion
of fish, baked in bread, or broiled on the fire,
and then came marinated fish, and some stewed with good spices,
all the choicest delicacies were there that he loved–
the knight said many times what a fine feast it was,
and they all quickly answered him in one voice:
"Fair friend,
accept this poor fare,
we shall give you better later!"
The knight made many jokes
for the wine made him merry.*

"Fair Friend,
This penance shall ye take,
It shall ye well amend!"
Much mirth the knight did make
For wine did gladness lend.

XVII

The hosts, in courteous wise the truth are fain to know
Of this, their goodly guest, if he his name will shew?
As courteously he quoth, he from that court did fare
Holden of good renown, where Arthur rule did bear,
(Rich, royal king was he) o'er all the Table Round-
And 't was Gawain himself who here had haven found,
Hither for Christmas come, as chance had ruled it right
Then when the lord had learned he had for guest that knight
Loudly be laughed for joy, he deemed such tidings good-
All men within the moat they waxed of mirthful mood
To think that they that tide should in his presence be
Who, for his prowess prized, and purest courtesie,
That doth to him belong, was prais'd everywhere,
Of all men upon earth none might with him compare.
Each to his fellow said, full softly, "Now shall we
The seemly fashion fair of courts full fitly see,
With faultless form of speech, and trick of noble word,
What charm in such may be that shall, unasked, be heard
Since here the father fine of courtesie we greet.
Methinks Christ sheweth us much grace, and favour meet,

*The hosts, who politely wanted to know the truth
asked their fine guest if he would tell them his name.
Just as politely he replied that he came from a court
of great fame, where Arthur ruled
(a rich and royal King) over the round table–
and it was Gawain who had found shelter here,
come here for Christmas, as chance would have it.
When the lord learned that he had that knight as his guest
he laughed loudly with joy, he thought that was fine news–
and everyone in the castle was happy
to think that at this time they should welcome one
who was so valued for his accomplishments and his courtesy
that he was praised everywhere,
so that there was no man on earth to compare with him.
Each man said quietly to his friend, "Now we shall see
how they behave in the greatest courts,
with faultless and noble speech,
we shall see without asking how charming it is
since here we are greeting the most courteous of men.
I think Christ is showing us great grace and favour
in giving us such a guest for Christmas as good Gawain:
when men like to sit around and sing, happy at His birth,
this knight shall teach us
the customs of courtesy
and maybe from his lips
we'll learn the speech of love."*

In granting us such guest for Yule as good Gawain:
When men, blithe for His birth, to sit, methinks, are fain,
and sing,
Customs of courtesie
This knight to us shall teach
And from his lips maybe
We'll learn of love the speech."

XVIII

By that was dinner done, the knight from table rose,
The eventide drew nigh, the day was near its close,
The chosen chaplains there to chapel go forthright,
Loudly the bells they ring, e'en as was fit and right.
To solemn evensong of this High Feast they go-
The lord the prayers would hear, his lady fair also,
To comely closet closed she entereth straightway;
And even so, full soon, follows Sir Gawain gay.
The lord his lappet took, and led him to a seat,
Hailing him by his name, in guise of friendship meet,
Of all knights in the world was he most welcome there
He thanked him, and the twain embrace with kisses fair,
And soberly they sit throughout the service high-
Then 't was the lady's will to see that knight with eye,
With many a maiden fair she cometh from her place,
Fairest was she in skin, in figure, and in face,
Of height and colour too, in every way so fair
That e'en Gaynore, the queen, might scarce with her compare.
She thro' the chancel came, to greet that hero good,
Led by another dame, who at her left hand stood;

With that dinner was finished, the knight rose from the table,
evening was coming, the day was nearly over,
and the chosen chaplains went straight to the chapel,
ringing the bells loudly as they should do.
They went to the solemn evensong of this great feast day—
the lord wanted to hear the prayers, and his fair lady also,
and she came at once into a handsome enclosed pew;
and merry Sir Gawain followed straight afterwards.
The lord took him by his coat and led him to a seat,
greeting him with friendship by his name,
saying that he was the most welcome there of all the knights in the world.
He thanked him, and the two embraced with sweet kisses,
and sat quietly throughout the great service—
then the lady wished to see the knight for herself,
and with her fair ladies she came from her place,
she was perfect of skin, figure and face,
in height and colour too, so perfect in every way
that even Guinevere, the queen, could hardly compare with her.
She came through the chancel, to meet that great hero,
led by another lady, who stood on her left;
she was older, and seemingly much respected,
she certainly had a good following of noblemen;

Older she was, I trow, and reverend seemingly,
With goodly following of nobles, verily;
But all unlike to sight, I trow, those ladies were,
Yellow, the older dame, whereas the first was
fair.
The cheeks of one were red, e'en as the rose
doth glow,
The other, wrinkles rough, in plenty, did she
shew.
The younger, kerchiefs soft, with many a pearl
so white,
Ware, that her breast and throat full well
displayed to sight,
Whiter they were than snow that on the hills
doth lie-
The other's neck was veiled in gorget folded
high,
That all her chin so black was swathed in milk-
white folds;
Her forehead all, I ween, in silk was rapped and
rolled,
Broidered it was full fair, adorned with knots
enow,
Till naught of her was seen save the black
bristly brow.
Her eyes, her nose, I ween, and eke her lips,
were bare
And those were ill to see, so bleared and sour
they were-
Meet mistress upon mold, so men might her
declare
that tide-
Short and thick-set was she,
Her hips were broad and wide,
And fairer far to see
The lady at her side.

XIX

When Gawain saw that dame, gracious of mien,
and gay,
Leave from his host he craved, and t'wards her
took his way;
The elder, bowing low, he fittingly doth greet,
Lightly within his arms he folds the lady sweet
Gives her a comely kiss, as fit from courteous
knight;

but those ladies were very different to look at;
the older one was yellow, while the first was
fair.
The cheeks of one were red, glowing like a rose,
while the other showed plenty of rough wrinkles.
The younger wore clothes that showed her
pearly white
breast and throat fully to the observer,
which were whiter than the snow on the hills–
the other one's neck was wrapped in a scarf,
so that her swarthy chin was covered with milky
white cloth;
her forehead too was muffled up in silk,
covered with fair embroidery, with ornaments
hanging from it,
so that nothing could be seen of her apart from
her black bristly brow.
Her eyes and nose, and also her lips, were bare
and they were unpleasant to see, they were so
bleary and dry–
but men still honoured her in that time–
she was short and thickset,
her hips were broad and wide,
and it was far sweeter to look at
the lady by her side.

When Gawain saw that lady, with her sweet
happy face,
he asked his host to excuse him, and went
towards her;
he greeted the older one fittingly with a low
bow,
and folded the sweet lady gently in his arms

She hailed him as her friend-a boon he prays forthright,
Her servant would he be, an so her will it were-
Betwixt the twain he walks, and, talking still, they fare
To hall, and e'en to hearth, and at the lord's command
Spices in plenty great are ready to their hand,
With wine that maketh gay at feast time, as is meet-
The lord, in laughing wise, he sprang unto his feet,
Bade them make mirth enow-all men his words must hear-
His hood he doffed from head, and hung it on a spear,
And quoth that that same man worship thereof should win
Who made the greatest mirth that Christmas-tide within:
"I'll fail not, by my faith, to frolic with the best,
Ere that my hood I lose-with help of every guest."
And thus, with joyous jest the lord doth try withal
To gladden Sir Gawain with games in this his hall
that night;
Till that the torches" flare
He needs must bid them light,
Gawain must from them fare
And seek his couch forthright.

XX

Then, on the morrow morn, when all men bear in mind
How our dear Lord was born to die for all mankind,
Joy in each dwelling dwells, I wot well, for His sake,
So did it there that day, when men High Feast would make;
For then, at every meal, messes, full richly dressed,
Men served upon the dais, with dainties of the best;

and gave her a sweet kiss, suitable for a courteous knight;
she greeted him as a friend; he immediately asked permission
to be her faithful servant, if she would allow it—
he walked between the two, and, still talking, they went
into the hall, up to the fire, and at the lord's command
there were plenty of spices waiting for them there
with wine to make the feast day merry, as it should be;
the lord, laughing, sprang to his feet,
and told them to be merry—everyone had to obey—
he threw his hood from his head, and hung it on a spear,
and challenged anyone to take it off him,
whoever was merriest at that Christmas time:
"I shall certainly make sure that I play with the best,
before I lose my hood—bring on every guest."
And so the lord tried to please Sir Gawain with merry jokes and games in his hall that night;
until he had to tell them
to light the torches,
and Gawain had to leave them
and go to bed.

Then, on the next morning, when all men remember
how our dear Lord was born to die for all humanity,
there was happiness in every dwelling for His sake,
and there was there that day, when the men wanted to celebrate;
men were served well spiced stews for every meal
on the dais, with the sweetest delicacies;
the old lady took the highest place,

That ancient lady there doth fill the highest seat,
The castle's lord, I trow, beside her, as was meet.
Sir Gawain hath his place beside that lady gay
At midmost of the board, when meat was served alway.
And then, thro' all the hall, each one, as seemed him best,
Sat, each in his degree-fitly they served each guest,
Much meat had they and mirth, with joy and merry song,
Methinks to tell thereof would take me over-long
Altho' perchance I strove to tell that tale as meet-
I wot well that Gawain, and this, the lady sweet,
In their fair fellowship much comfort needs must find,
In the dear dalliance of words and glances kind,
And converse courteous, from all unfitness free-
Such pastime fitting were for prince in purity-
Sweet strain
Of trump and piping clear
And drum, doth sound amain;
Each doth his minstrel hear,
And even so the twain.

XXI

Much mirth they made that day, and e'en the morrow's morn
Nor slackened of the feast when the third day was born;
The joy of sweet Saint John, gentle it was to hear,
The folk, they deemed the feast fast to its end drew near;
(The guests must needs depart, e'en in the dawning grey)
Full early did they rise, and serve the wine straightway;
Danced carols merrily, so, blithe, the day they passed,
And when the hour waxed late they took their leave at last.
Each one to wend his way whenas the day

with the lord of the castle beside her, as was fitting.
Sir Gawain had his place beside the lovely lady at the middle of the table, where the meat was first served.
And then the others sat around the hall, each one in what seemed the best place according to his station; each guest was served, and they had much food and laughter, with joy and happy songs, and I think it would take me too long to describe it all, if I tried to really do it justice; I certainly know that Gawain and this sweet lady took great happiness from their sweet friendship, exchanging fair words and glances, talking courteously, with no vulgarity, a pastime suitable for a pure prince: sweet music of trumpets and pipes and drums sounded all around; everyone listened to the singers, and so did those two.

They had much fun that day, and even on the next day, and the feast didn't slacken off when the third day came; it was wonderful to hear the rejoicing on St John's day, then people decided the feast was quickly coming to its end; (the guests had to leave, even in the grey dawn) they got up very early, and served wine at once; they danced merrily to carols and spent the day happily, and when it got late they said goodbye at last. Each one wanted to make his way before daybreak– Gawain wanted to say goodbye; the lord took him by the hand

should break-
Gawain would bid good-day-his hand the lord
doth take
To his own chamber leads, and by the chimney
wide,
To thank his guest full fain, he draweth him
aside;
Thanks him for worship fair that he from him
had won,
And for the honour high he to his house had
done
By lending countenance unto this Christmas
Feast-
"Of honours, while I live, I 'll count this not the
least
That Gawain this, my guest, at Christ's own
Feast hath been!"
"Gramercy," quoth Gawain, "In all good faith, I
ween
The honour it is yours, and may Christ you
repay.
I wait upon your word, to do your will alway
As I be bound thereto by night and e'en by day
of right-"
The lord, he was full fain
To keep with him the knight,
Then answered him Gawain
That he in no wise might.

XXII

The lord, he courteous prayed that he would tell
him there
What deed of daring drove Gawain afar to fare
E'en at this time from court, and thus alone to
wend,
Before this Holy Feast had come unto an end?
"In sooth, Sir," quoth the knight, "Ye speak the
truth alway,
A hasty quest, and high, doth send me on my
way,
For I myself must seek, and find, a certain place
And whitherward to wend I wot not, by God's
grace!
Nor would I miss my tryst at New Year, by my
soul,

*and lead him to his own chamber, and by the
wide chimney breast
he took his guest aside to thank him properly;
to thank him for the kindness he had shown him,
and the great honour he had done to his house
by agreeing to join in the Christmas feast;
"As long as I live this shall be one of my
greatest honours,
that Gawain was my guest at Christmas time!"
"By heaven," said Gawain, "I swear to you I
think
it is you who deserves honour, and I hope Christ
repays you.
I wait for your orders, I will always do what you
want,
I am at your service both day and night."
The lord was very keen
to keep the knight with him,
but Gawain answered
there was no way he could stay.*

*The lord politely asked him to tell him
what daring adventure had brought Gawain so
far
from the court at this time, travelling alone,
before Christmas had come to an end?
"You're certainly right it's unusual, sir," said
the knight,
"it's a great quest I'm undertaking and I must
do it soon, I must find a certain place
and I have no idea how I'm going to get there!
I swear I would not miss my appointment at New
Year
for all the land of Logres! May Christ help me!
So Sir Host, I must ask you to tell me truthfully
if you have ever heard
of the Green Chapel? Where is such a place?*

For all the land of Logres! Christ help me to my goal!
Therefore Sir Host, I now require ye without fail
To tell me here in truth if ye e'er heard a tale
Told of a Chapel Green? Where such a place may be?
The knight who keepeth it, green too, I ween, is he;
We sware a forward fast, I trow, between us twain,
That I that man would meet, might I thereto attain,
And to that same New Year but few days now remain-
Now fainer far would I behold that self-same knight,
If so it were God's will, than any gladder sight;
Therefore with your good will, I needs must wend my way
Since I have, for my quest, but three bare days alway;
Fainer were I to die than fail in this my quest-"
Then, laughing, quoth the lord: "Of needs must be my guest,
I 'll shew to thee thy goal ere yet the term be o'er
That very Chapel Green-so vex thy soul no more,
Do thou in bed abide and take thine ease, I pray,
Until the fourth day dawn, with New Year go thy way
And thou shalt reach thy goal ere yet it be midday.
So, still,
To the New Year abide
Then rise, thy goal is near
Men shall thee thither guide,
"T is not two miles from here-"

XXIII

Sir Gawain, he was glad, and laughed out gay and free,
"I thank ye, Sire, for this, o'er all your courtesie,
Achieved is this my quest, and I shall, at your will
Within your burg abide, and do your pleasure

The knight who guards it is also green;
we made a pact between the two of us
that I would go there to meet this man,
and it's only a few days until the New Year;
I would rather see that knight, if
God permits it, than anything else;
so with your permission I must go,
as I have only three short days left for my quest;
I would rather die than not complete it."
Then the lord said, laughing: "you must stay as my guest,
I'll show you your goal before your time is up,
that Green Chapel, so don't torture yourself,
stay in bed and rest, I pray,
until the morning of the fourth day, and on New Year
you can go on your way and you will reach your goal before midday.
So, stay here until the New Year,
then go, your goal is near.
Men shall guide you there,
it's not two miles away."

Sir Gawain was glad and laughed out freely and happily,
"I thank you, sir, for this, more than all your other kindness,
I have achieved my aim, and I will, with your permission,

still."
The lord, he took that knight, and set him at his side,
And bade the ladies come to cheer them at that tide,
Tho' they had, of themselves, fair solace, verily-
The host, for very joy, he jested merrily
As one for meed of mirth scarce wist what he might say.
Then, turning to the knight, he cried on him alway:
"Didst swear to do the deed I should of thee request,
Now art thou ready here to hearken my behest?"
"Yea, Sire, forsooth am I," so quoth that hero true
"While in your burg I bide, servant am I to you!"
"Now," quoth the host, "methinks, your travail sore hath been,
Here hast thou waked with me, nor had thy fill, I ween,
Of sustenance, or sleep,-an thou thine host wouldst please
Thou shalt lie long in bed, and, lingering, take thine ease
At morn, nor rise for mass, but eat as thou shalt say
E'en when thou wilt, my wife with thee a while shall stay
And solace thee with speech, till I my homeward way
have found.
For I betimes shall rise,
A-hunting am I bound."
Gawain, this, his device
Doth grant him at that stound.

XXIV

"First," quoth the host, "we'll make a forward fair and free,
Whate'er in wood I win the profit thine shall be,
What cheer thou shalt achieve, shalt give me, 'gainst my gain;
Now swear me here with truth to keep this 'twixt us twain

stay in your castle and do what you wish."
The lord took that knight and put him by his side,
and told the ladies to come and celebrate with them,
although they had been having a fine time by themselves;
the host in his merriment made so many jokes he seemed like someone so happy he hardly knew what he was saying.
Then, turning to the knight, he spoke loudly to him:
"You swore to do what I would ask you, now are you ready to listen to my wishes?"
"Yes, sir, I certainly am," said that noble hero, "while I am in your castle, I am your servant!"
"Now," said the host, "I think you have had a hard journey,
and you have stayed awake with me and not had, I think,
enough food or sleep yet; you can please your host
by staying late in bed, and, resting, do nothing in the morning, nor get up for mass, but eat whenever you want, my wife will stay with you while
and entertain you with conversation, until I come home.
For I shall get up early,
I'm going hunting."
Gawain agreed to this with a bow.

"Now," said the host, "let's make an agreement; whatever I find in the woods will belong to you, and you will exchange it for whatever good things you find here.
Swear to me you'll keep this bargain between us whatever happens, for good or for ill."
"By God," said good Gawain, "I agree to this,

Whate'er our hap may be, or good or ill befall.-"
"By God," quoth good Gawain, "I grant ye this withal,
An such play pleaseth you, forsooth it pleaseth me-"
"Now, bring the beverage here, the bargain set shall be."
So quoth the castle's lord, and each one laughed, I trow,
They drank and dallied there and dealt with sport enow,
Those lords and ladies fair, e'en as it liked them best,
And so, in friendship fair, with many a courteous jest,
They stood, and stayed awhile, and spake with softest speech,
Then kissed at parting, e'en as courtesy doth teach.
And then, with service fit, and many a torch alight,
Unto his bed at last they brought each gallant knight
again-
Yet ere their couch they sought
The cov'nant 'twixt the twain
The lord to memory brought,
For jesting was he fain.

if such games please you, then they please me as well."
"Now, bring the drinks here, and we'll seal the bargain,"
said the lord of the castle, and each of them laughed;
they drank and played there and had much fun,
these fair lords and ladies, in the way they liked best,
and so they stayed there for a while in friendship
with many courtly jokes, and spoke sweetly to each other,
then they kissed on parting, as is right by the rules of courtesy.
And then with excellent servants and many torches
each gallant knight went to his bed;
but before they found their rest
the bargain between the two
was repeated by the lord,
for he was not joking.

Book Three

I

Full early ere 't was day the folk arise withal,
The guests would go their way-upon their grooms they call,
They busk them busily to saddle each good steed,
The girths they tighten there, and truss the mails at need.
The nobles, ready all, in riding gear arrayed,
Leapt lightly to their steeds, their hand on bridle laid;
Each wight upon his way doth at his will ride fast-
The lord of all the land, I wot, was not the last,
Ready for riding he, with his men, at that same
Ate a sop hastily whenas from mass they came.
With blast of bugle bold forth upon bent he 'ld go,
Ere yet the day had dawned on the cold earth below.
He and his knights bestrode, each one, their horses high.
The huntsmen couple then the hounds right speedily.
Then, calling on the dogs, unclose the kennel door;
A bugle blast they blow, but three notes, and no more.
Loudly the brachets bay, and wake the echoes there,
They check their hounds so good who to the chase would fare
A hundred men all told, so doth the tale declare ride fast;
The trackers on the trail
The hounds, uncoupled, cast,
Thro' forest, hill and dale
Rings loud the bugle blast.

Before sunrise the company rose,
the guests who were leaving called for the grooms,
who hurried to saddle each good horse,
tightening the girths and packing their bags.
The nobles were all ready, dressed in their riding gear,
they sprang onto their horses and took hold of the reins;
each one went quickly on the road he chose;
the lord of the land was not the last one to mount,
he and his men were ready for riding, eating a quick snack after they came from mass.
With the sound of a horn he headed out before the sun had risen on the cold earth.
He and his knights each mounted on their high horses.
Before sunrise the huntsmen put leashes on their dogs
and called them, unbolting the door of the kennels;
they blew a blast on the horn, just three notes, no more.
The hounds bayed loudly and roused the echoes, and the ones who were hunting brought them into line;
a hundred swift riders there were, the story goes;
the huntsmen were on the trail,
the unleashed hounds looked for the scent,
and the loud bugle blast blew through the forest, hill and dale.

II

At the first warning note that bade the hunt awake
The deer within the dale for dread they needs must quake;
Swift to the heights they hie-but soon must turn about,

The first warning note that rose the hounds terrified the deer in the woods and they rushed to the hills, but soon they had to turn, as the beaters shouted at them so loudly.
The stags with their splendid spreading antlers

The men in ambush hid so loud they cry and shout.
The harts, with heads high-held, they pass in safety there,
E'en so the stately stags with spreading antlers fair,
(For so the lords' command at close time of the year
That none should lift his hand save 'gainst the female deer.)
The hinds with "Hag" and "War" they hold the lines within,
The does are driven back to dale with deafening din;
Swift as they speed, I trow, fair shooting might ye see,
The arrows striking true as 'neath the boughs they flee;
Their broad heads deeply wound, and, smitten on the flank,
The bleeding deer they fall, dying, upon the bank.
The hounds, in hasty course, follow upon the trail,
Huntsmen, with sounding horns, for speed they do not fail,
Follow with ringing cries that cliffs might cleave in twain;
The deer that "scape the darts, they by the dogs are ta'en,
Run down, and riven, and rent, within the bounds so wide,
Harassed upon the hill, worried by waterside;
The men well knew their craft of forest and of flood,
The greyhounds were full swift to follow thro' the wood,
They caught them ere the men with arrows, as they stood,
could smite-
The lord was glad and gay,
His lance he wielded light,
With joy he passed the day
Till fell the shades of night.

and the bucks with their heads held high passed safely
(for it was the order of the lord that only female deer should be killed in the close season).
The hinds were held back with cries of "Hey!" and "Woah!",
The deafening racket drove the does back to the dale;
as fast as they went you could see good shooting,
the arrows striking home as they fled beneath the branches;
the broad arrowheads struck deeply and, wounded in the side,
the bleeding deer fell, dying, on the bank.
The hounds swiftly followed upon the trail,
and the huntsmen were not left behind with their blowing horns,
following with loud cries that might have split the cliffs in half;
the deer that escaped the arrows were captured by the dogs,
run down, scratched and torn within that wide country,
hounded on the hill, worried by the waterside;
the men were experts both in forests and by the water,
and the greyhounds chased swiftly through the woods,
they caught them before the men with arrows could shoot;
the lord was happy and gay,
wielding his light spear,
he passed the day happily
until nightfall.

III

The lord, he maketh sport beneath the woodland bough,
Sir Gawain, that good knight, in bed he lieth now,
Hiding, while daylight gleamed upon the walls without,
'Neath costly cov'ring fair, curtained all round about.
As he half slumbering lay, it seem'd to his ear
A small sound at his door all sudden must he hear;
His head a little raised above the covering soft,
He grasps the curtain's edge, and lifteth it aloft,
And waiteth warily to wot what fate may hold-
It was the lady fair, most lovely to behold!
Gently she drew the door behind her, closing tight,
And came toward the couch-shamed was that gallant knight,
He laid him lightly down, and made as tho' he slept;
So stole she to his side, and light and soft she stept,
The curtain upward cast, within its fold she crept,
And there upon his bed her seat she soft doth take
Waiting in patience still until that he awake.
Cautious and quiet, awhile the knight, half hidden, lay,
And in his conscience conned the case with care alway;
What might the meaning be? He marvelled much, I trow,
Yet quoth within himself: "It were more seemly now
To speak with gentle speech, ask what her will may be,
So made he feint to wake, and turned him presently
Lifted his eyelids then, and stared, as in amaze,
Made of the Cross the sign, that so his words and ways
be wise-
Her chin and cheeks are sweet
In red and white devise,

So the lord hunted under the eaves of the forest, while Sir Gawain, that good knight, lay in bed resting beneath fine blankets, surrounded by curtains, while daylight shone on the walls outside.
As he lay half asleep he thought that he suddenly heard a small sound at his door; he poked his head a little way out of the soft coverings and took hold of the edge of the curtain, and lifted it up, and waited warily to see what fate was bringing: it was the fair lady, lovely to see!
She softly closed the door behind her, shutting it tight, and came towards the bed; that gallant knight was embarrassed, and pretended he was asleep; so she sneaked to his side, stepping softly, lifted the curtain and crept inside, and she took her seat quietly on his bed waiting patiently until he woke.
Cautious and quiet the knight lay hidden for a while, as he carefully examined the business with his conscience; what might it mean? He was astonished, but he said to himself: "it would be more proper now to politely ask her what she wants."
So he pretended to wake up, and turned over at once, opened his eyes and stared as if astonished, made the sign of the cross in hope that his words and actions would be wise; her chin and cheeks were sweet, mixing red and white, She graciously greeted him, with laughing lips and eyes.

Gracious, she doth him greet
With laughing lips and eyes.

IV

"Good-morrow, Sir Gawain," so spake the lady fair,
"A careless sleeper ye, I came ere ye were ware,
Now are ye trapped and ta'en, as ye shall truly know,
I 'll bind ye in your bed ere that ye hence should go!"
Laughing, the lady lanced her jests at him alway,
Sir Gawain answered blithe: "Give ye good-morrow gay,
Know I am at your will, (forsooth it pleaseth me)
And here for grace I yearn, yielding me readily.
For where one needs must yield to do so swift were best!"
And thus he answer made, with many a merry jest;
"But might I, Lady fair, find grace before your eyes,
Then loose, I pray, your bonds, and bid your prisoner rise,
I 'ld get me from this bed, and better clad, I trow,
I in your converse kind comfort would find enow."
"Nay, nay, forsooth, beau Sire," so quoth that lady sweet,
"Ye shall not rise from bed, I 'll rede ye counsel meet,
For I shall hold ye here, since other may not be,
And talk with this my knight, who captive is to me,
For well I know, in sooth, ye are that same Gawain
Worshipped by all the world where ye to fare be fain;
For all your honour praise, your gracious courtesie,
Or lords or ladies fair, all men on earth that be!
Now are ye here, I wis, and all alone we twain,
My lord to fare afield with his free folk is fain,

"Good morning, Sir Gawain," said the fair lady,
"you are a careless sleeper, I came before you knew,
and you are now trapped and captured, as you will find out,
I'll tie you to your bed before I'll let you go away!"
Laughing, the lady teased him with her jokes.
Sir Gawain answered blithely: "A very good morning to you,
you should know I'm at your orders (which very much pleases me)
and I hope for mercy, I surrender willingly,
for when one has to surrender it's best to do it quickly!"
And so he answered her, with many merry jokes;
"But if fair Lady you agree to be merciful,
then I pray you to untie your bonds and tell your prisoner to get up,
I'll get out of this bed and I think I could enjoy your
conversation more if I was properly dressed."
"No, no, not at all, sweet Sir," said that lovely lady,
"you shall not get out of bed, I have another plan for you,
for I shall keep you here as there is no one else,
and talk with this knight of mine, my prisoner,
for I know very well that you are the same Gawain
who is worshipped by all the world wherever you go;
everyone praises your honour, your sweet courtesy,
whether it's lords or fair ladies, everyone on earth!
And now you are here, and we too are alone,
my Lord has gone hunting with his freemen,
the men are still in bed, and so are my women—
the door is safely shut, and locked as well;
since I have the one whom all men praise in my power,

The men, they lie abed, so do my maidens all-
The door is safely shut, and closed and hasped
withal;
Since him whom all men praise I in my hand
hold fast,
I well will use my time the while the chance
doth last!
Now rest,
My body's at your will
To use as ye think best,
Perforce, I find me still
Servant to this my guest!"

I will take my opportunity while I have the
chance!
Now rest, my body is at your service
to use however you think best,
because I find I am still
a servant to my guest!"

V

"In good faith," quoth Gawain, "I now bethink
me well,
I be not such an one as this your tale would tell!
To reach such reverence as ye rehearse but now
I all unworthy were-that do I soothly vow!
Yet, God wot, I were glad, an so ye thought it
good,
If I in word and deed here at your service stood;
To pleasure this your prayer, a pure joy 't were
to me."
"In good faith, Sir Gawain," the lady answered
free,
"The prowess and the praise that please us ladies
fair
I lack not, nor hold light, but little gain it were
Ladies there be enow to whom it were more
dear
To hold their knight in hold, e'en as I hold ye
here,
To dally daintily with courteous words and fair
That bring them comfort good, and cure them of
their care,
Than wealth of treasure told, or gold they own
withal-
But now I praise the Lord who here upholdeth
all
Him whom they all desire is in my hold and hall
of grace!"
She made him such good cheer
That lady fair of face,
The knight was fain to hear
And answer, in his place.

"I swear," said Gawain, "I am very sure
that I am not the man you're talking about!
To be praised in the way you just have,
I am unworthy of it, I swear!
But God knows I would be pleased if you agreed
to let my speech and deeds be at your service;
it would be the greatest happiness to me to
answer your prayers."
"I swear, Sir Gawain," the lady freely
answered,
"it would be rude of me to think lightly of the
things
that everybody else praises so highly;
there are plenty of ladies who would be
delighted
to have you in their power, as I have you here,
to exchange pleasantries with sweet and
courteous words
to give themselves comfort, and ease their
burdens,
they would prefer it to a great treasure, all the
gold they own–
but now I praise the Lord who directs everything
on earth
that the one they all desire is here, my
prisoner!"
She was so sweet to him,
that beautiful lady,
the knight was glad to listen,
and answer appropriately.

VI

He quoth: "Now Mary Maid reward ye, as she may,
I find your frankness fair and noble, sooth to say.
Full many folk, I trow, have well entreated me,
Yet greater honour far than all their courtesie
I count your praise, who naught save goodness here shall know."
"By Mary Maid," she quoth, "methinks it is not so,
For were my worth above all women who may live,
And all of this world's wealth were in mine hand to give,
And I were free of choice a lord to choose to me,
Then, for the customs good I in this knight must see,
For beauty debonaire, for bearing blithe and gay,
For all that I have heard, and hold for truth alway,
Upon no man on mold save ye my choice were laid."
"I wot well," quoth the knight, "a better choice ye made!
Yet am I proud of this, the praise, ye give to me,
My sovereign ye, and I your servant, verily,
Do yield me here your knight, and may Christ ye repay!"
They spake of many things till noon had passed away,
And aye the lady made mien that she loved him well,
And aye he turned aside her sweet words as they fell,
For were she brightest maid of maidens to his mind,
The less love would he shew, since loss he thought to find
anon-
The blow that should him slay,
And for his blow was boon-
The lady leave did pray.
He granted her, full soon.

He said: "Now may the Virgin Mary reward you,
I must tell you I think your generosity is sweet and noble.
Many people have treated me well,
but your praise means much more to me,
however little it's deserved."
"By the Virgin Mary," she said, "I don't think that's the case,
if I was better than all women alive,
and all the wealth of the world was mine to give,
and I had my free choice of husband,
then, for the good deportment I seen this knight,
for sweet beauty, for attractive bearing,
and everything that I've heard, and can see is true,
I would not choose any man on earth but you."
"I know well," said the knight, "that you made a better choice!
And yet I am proud to be praised like this by you,
you're my queen, and I'm your servant, truly,
let me be your knight, and may Christ reward you!"
They spoke of many things until it was past noon,
and the lady behaved as if she loved him deeply,
and he always avoided her compliments as she gave them,
for he thought she was the loveliest of all women,
and so showed her no love, as he knew he could not have her;
soon he would have to face the fatal blow,
in return for the one he gave;
the lady asked to leave,
and he agreed at once.

VII

Then, as she gave "good-day," she laughed with glance so gay,
And, standing, spake a word that 'stonied him alway:
"May He who speedeth speech reward thee well, I trow,
But that ye be Gawain I much misdoubt me now,"-
"And wherefore?" quoth the knight in fashion frank and fair
Fearing lest he have failed in custom debonaire:
The lady blessed him then, and spake as in this wise:
"Gawain so good a knight is holden in all eyes,
So clad in courtesie is he, in sooth, that ne'er
Had he thus holden speech for long with lady fair
But he had craved a kiss by this, his courtesie,
Or trifling token ta'en at end of converse free!"
Then quoth Gawain: "Ywis, if this ye fitting deem
I 'll kiss at your command, as doth a knight beseem
Who tarrieth to ask, and doth refusal fear-"
She clasped him in her arms, e'en as she stood anear,
Lightly she bent adown, and kissed that knight so free,
Commending him to Christ, as he her, courteously-
Then, without more ado, forth from the door she went;
The knight made haste to rise, on speed was he intent,
He called his chamberlain, his robes he chose anon,
When he was fitly garbed to mass he blithe has gone;
Then sat him down to meat, 't was served in fitting guise,
Merry he passed the day, and, till the moon did rise
made game-
Better was never knight
Entreated of fair dame

Then, as she said "goodbye," she laughed and gave him a merry glance,
and as she stood she said words that astonished him:
"I'm sure the Lord will give you great rewards, but now I'm doubtful that you are actually Gawain,"
"And why is that?" asked the knight, boldly and politely,
worried that he might have been bad mannered: then the lady blessed him, and said this:
"Gawain is such a good knight in everybody's opinion,
with such excellent knightly manners that he never
could have spoken for this long with a beautiful lady
without asking for a kiss or
some sort of token at the end of such excellent conversation!"
Then Gawain said: "Certainly, if you think it's right,
I will kiss at your order, as is suitable for a knight
who was slow to ask, fearing refusal–"
She held him in arms, standing close to him,
she gently bent down and kissed that knight openly,
asking Christ to protect him, and he asked the same, courteously;
then, with no more ado, she went out of the door;
the knight quickly got up, he meant to move fast,
he called for his servant, chose his clothes,
and when he was properly dressed he happily went to mass;
then he sat down to eat, and was well served,
and he passed the day happily, entertaining himself until the moonrise;
no knight was ever treated
so well by beautiful ladies,
both the old and the young,
than he was at that time.

Old, or of beauty bright,
Than he was, at that same.

VIII

And aye the lord in land finds sport unto his mind,
Hunting o'er hill and heath, chasing the barren hind,
So many hath he slain, ere yet the sun was low,
Of does, and other deer, a wonder 't was to know.
The folk together flock, whenas the end drew near
Quickly a quarry make of all the slaughtered deer;
The best, they bowed thereto, with many a knight to aid,
The fairest hinds of grease together they have laid,
Set them to quartering there, e'en as the need doth ask,
The fat was set aside by those who knew their task,
From all uncleanness freed, the flesh they sever there,
The chest they slit, and draw the erber forth with care;
With knife both sharp and keen the neck they next divide,
Then sever all four limbs, and strip off fair the hide.
The belly open slit, the bowels aside they lay,
With swift strokes of the knife the knot they cut away;
They grip the gargiloun, and speedily divide
Weasand and wind-pipe then, the guts are cast aside,
The shoulder-blade around, with blade so sharp and keen,
They cut, and leave the side whole and untouched, I ween.
The breast they deftly carve, the halves they lie a-twin,
And with the gargiloun their work they now begin;
They rip it swiftly up, and take it clean away,

And still the lord of the land was occupied with his sport,
hunting over hills and heaths, chasing the barren hind,
before sunset he had killed so many
does and other deer it was astonishing.
The hunters gathered together as the day came to an end
and they quickly piled up all their slaughtered deer;
all the knights gathered round and chose the best ones,
setting them to one side,
and they started butchering them in the proper manner;
the fat was set aside by those who knew their business,
and now that it was clean they cut open the flesh,
slit the chest and carefully drew out the gullet;
with a sharp knife they next split the neck,
cut off all four limbs, and stripped off the hide.
Opening the belly they lay the bowels aside,
and with swift strokes of the knife they detached them;
they gripped the throat and quickly divided
the oesophagus and windpipe, threw the guts aside,
cut around the shoulder blade with a sharp blade,
leaving the whole flank in one piece.
They skilfully carved the breast into two halves,
and began their work with the throat;
they swiftly cut it and lifted it clean out,
pulled out the offal and then at once
they neatly cut the skin between the ribs
until they had the whole of the backbone bare.
Then they came to the haunch,
lifting it in one piece and cleanly cutting it off,
and taking out the heart and liver,
then, where the thighs join,
they cut the flaps from behind,

Void the avancers out, and then, methinks, straightway
The skin betwixt the ribs they cut in fashion fair
Till they have left them all e'en to the backbone bare.
So come they to the haunch, that doth belong thereto,
They bear it up all whole, and cleanly cut it thro'
That, with the numbles, take, alike they be the two,
of kind
Then, where the thighs divide
The flaps they cut behind,
And thus, on either side,
Thighs from the back unbind.

and so on either side
they freed the thighs from the back.

IX

Then head and neck alike, they hew them off with heed,
The sides from off the chine are sundered now with speed.
The corbie's fee they cast into the wood hard by,
Each thick side thro' the ribs they pierce it, verily,
And hang them all aloft, fixed to the haunches fair-
Each fellow for his fee doth take as fitting there.
Then, on a deer's skin spread, they give the hounds their food.
The liver, lights, and paunch, to keep the custom good,
And bread soaked in the blood they scatter 'mid the pack-
The hounds, they bay amain, nor bugle blast doth lack.
Thus, with the venison good, they take the homeward way,
Sounding upon their horns a merry note and gay.
By that, the day was done, the folk, with eventide,
That comely castle sought, wherein their guest doth bide
full still-
To bliss and firelight bright

Then they quickly chopped off the head and neck,
and separated both flanks from the nape.
They threw meat for the crows into the nearby woods,
and pierced each flank through the ribs
and hung it up high, fixed by the legs;
every man took his fair share.
Then, spread over deerskin, they fed their hounds;
the liver, offal and stomach, in the usual way,
and also bread soaked in blood they threw to the pack;
the hounds bayed and the horns blew.
So with the good venison they made their way home,
blowing a merry note upon their horns.
The day was over and with the evening the people
looked for the comfortable castle where their guest still was:
the lord is coming home
to comfort and bright firelight
to meet that good knight;
they had had a wonderful time!

The lord is come at will;
To meet that goodly knight-
Of joy they had their fill!

X

Then at the lord's command, the folk they
thither call,
Quickly the ladies come, and maidens, one and
all,
And there before the folk he bids his men
straightway,
The venison they have brought before them all
to lay.
And then, in goodly jest, he calleth Sir Gawain,
The tale of that day's sport he to rehearse is fain,
Shews him how fair the fat upon the ribs, sharp
shorn,
And quoth: "How seemeth this? Have I won
praise this morn?
Am I, thro' this my craft, worthy of praise from
thee?"
"Yea, soothly," quoth Gawain, "the fairest game
I see
That I in winter-time have seen this seven year!"
"And all this," quoth his host, "Gawain, I give
thee here
By covenant and accord, the whole thou well
may'st claim."
"'T is sooth," then said the knight, "I grant ye at
this same.
Won have I worthily a prize, these walls within
Which, with as good a will, ye now from me
must win."
With that he clasps his arms around his neck so
fair
And in right comely wise he kissed him then
and there,
"Now here hast thou my gain, no more hath
fallen to me-
I trow had it been more my gift were none less
free!"
"'T is good," quoth the good knight, "nor shall
my thanks be slow
Yet might it better be, an I the truth might know,
Where thou didst win this grace, or by thy wit or
no?"

Then at the lord's command they called all
people there,
the ladies came quickly, and all the girls,
and in front of his people he told his men at
once
to lay the venison they had brought in front of
them.
And then, in a jolly mood, he called Sir Gawain,
to tell him the story of the day's hunting;
he showed him how thick the fat on the ribs was,
and said: "What do you think of this? Have I
done well this morning?
Do my skills deserve to be praised by you?"
"Yes, indeed," Sir Gawain, "this is the best
game
I have seen in winter for seven years!"
"And all of this," said his host, "I give to you,
Gawain,
by the terms of our agreement, you can have it
all."
Then the knight said, "I must repay you.
I have won a good prize inside these walls,
which, in the same spirit, you must have from
me."
With that he threw his arms around his
handsome neck
and in a sweet way he kissed him then and
there;
"Now you have my prize, I found no more;
I promise if there have been more you would
have it!"
"It's good," said the good knight, "and I give
you thanks,
but it might be better, if I knew the truth,
of where you won this prize, and how you got
it?"
"Ask no more," said Gawain, "this was our
agreement;
since you've taken your reward you can't ask for
more."
They laughed and made merry,

"Ask no more," quoth Gawain, "so did our forward stand,"
Since ye have ta'en your right no more may ye demand."
At will
They laughed and made them gay
With many a jest I trow,
To supper go straightway,
With dainties new enow.

with many happy jokes,
and went straight into supper,
with plenty of new delicacies.

XI

Then by the hearth they sit, on silken cushions soft,
And wine, within those walls, I wot, they serve full oft,
And, ever, as they jest, come morrow morn, they say
That forward they 'll fulfil which they had kept to-day.
What chance soe'er betide, they will exchange their gain
When they at nightfall meet, be much or little ta'en.
This covenant they accord, in presence of the court,
And beverage to the board at that same time was brought,
A courteous leave, at last, doth each from other take,
And each man for his bed himself doth ready make.
The cock at early morn, had crowed and cackled thrice
When swift, the lord arose, with him his knights of price;
They hearken mass, and meat, with service fit, they bring,
Then forth to forest fare ere yet the day doth spring
for chace-
With sound of hunter's horns
O'er plain they swiftly pace,
Uncoupled midst the thorns
Each hound doth run on race.

Then they sat by the hearth, on silken cushions,
and I know they had plenty of wine,
and they joked with each other that the next day
they would keep the same bargain they had kept today.
Whatever fate should bring them, they would exchange their prizes
when they met at nightfall, whether they were great or small.
They made this agreement in the presence of the court
and at the same time drinks were brought to the table,
and at last they said a sweet goodnight to each other,
and each man got himself ready for bed.
In the early morning the clock had crowed three times
when the lord quickly arose with his finest knights;
they heard mass and then were served with meat,
then set out to hunt in the forest before the day had broken;
with the sound of hunter's horns
they swiftly galloped over the plain,
and let free amidst the woods
each hound rushed on.

XII

Full soon they strike the scent, hard by a rock withal,
Huntsmen cheer on those hounds who first upon it fall,
Loudly, with whirling words, and clamour rising high,
The hounds that heard the call haste hither at the cry.
Fast on the scent they fall, full forty at that tide,
Till of the pack the cry was heard both far and wide.
So fiercely rose their bay, the rocks, they rang again,
The huntsmen with their horns to urge them on were fain.
Then, sudden, all the pack together crowd and cry
Before a thicket dense, beneath a crag full high,
Hard by the water's edge-the pack, with one consent,
Run to the rugged rocks, which lie all scarred and rent.
Hounds to the finding fare, the men, they follow keen,
And cast about the crag, and rocks that lie between.
The knights, full well they knew what beast had here its lair
And fain would drive it forth before the bloodhounds there.
Then on the bush they beat, and bid the game uprise-
With sudden rush across the beaters, out there hies
A great and grisly boar, most fearsome to behold,
The herd he long had left, for that he waxed full old.
Of beast, and boar, methinks, biggest and fiercest he,
I trow me at his grunt full many grieved must be;
Three at the first assault prone on the earth he threw,
And sped forth at best speed, nor other harm they knew.

They soon picked up a scent, close by a rock,
and the huntsmen urged on the hounds who first found it,
loudly, with a great commotion,
the hounds that heard the call hurried there.
They quickly picked up the scent, at least forty of them,
until the whole pack heard that cry.
Their baying was so fierce that the rocks rang with it,
and the huntsmen urged them on with their horns.
Then, suddenly, the pack crowded together
in front of a dense thicket, beneath a tall crag,
by the edge of the water; the pack ran as one
to the rough rocks, which were all scarred and broken.
The men followed their hounds quickly
and searched around the crag and the rocks.
The knights knew very well what beast was hiding there,
and wanted to drive it in front of the bloodhounds.
They beat on the bush to drive out the game;
suddenly out past the beaters there came
a huge grizzled boar, terrifying to see,
he had long ago left the herd, for he was ancient.
He was, I think, the biggest and fiercest boar ever,
and I think many were going to suffer through him.
With his first attack he threw three down on the ground,
then rushed on without pausing to do more harm.
Then the knights shouted "Hey! Hey!",
And the huntsmen blew shrill notes on their horns;
at that time there was a wonderful noise of men and dogs
who chased after the boar–loudly calling out to kill him;
he fought back against the hounds
as they cornered him,
they yelped and whined loudly

Then Hey! and Hey! the knights halloo with shout and cry,

Huntsmen with horn to mouth send forth shrill notes and high,

Merry the noise of men and dogs, I ween, that tide

Who followed on the boar-with boastful shout they cried

to stay-

The hounds' wrath would he quell

Oft as he turned to bay,

Loudly they yelp and yell,

His tusks they tare alway.

XIII

The men make ready then their arrows sharp and keen,

The darts they swiftly fly, oft is he hit, I ween,

But never point may pierce, nor on his hide have hold,

And never barb may bite his forehead's fearsome fold.

The shafts are splintered there, shivered, they needs must fall,

The heads, they bit indeed, yet but rebound withal.

But when he felt the blows, tho' harmless all they fell,

Then, mad for rage, he turned, and 'venged him passing well;

He rushed upon the knights, and wounded them full sore

Until, for very fear, they fled his face before.

The lord, on steed swift-paced, doth follow on his track,

Blowing his bugle loud, nor valour doth he lack,

Thus thro' the wood he rides, his horn rings loud and low,

Upon the wild boar's track until the sun was low.

And so the winter's day he passeth on this wise

The while his goodly guest in bed, 'neath covering lies,

Sir Gawain bides at home-In gear of rich devise and hue,

The dame made no delay

as he tore at them with his tusks.

The men got their short sharp pointed arrows ready,
the darts flew swiftly and he was often hit,
but they never went in or stuck in his skin,
and no point ever got through his thick forehead.
The shafts splintered and shattered, they had to fall out,
the heads did bite in but then bounced out.
But when he felt the blows, although they were harmless,
mad with rage he turned and took great revenge;
he rushed at the knights and gave them many wounds
until, terrified, they ran away from him.
The lord, on a fast horse, followed on his track,
loudly blowing his bugle, he wasn't lacking courage,
and he rode through the woods with his horn sounding out,
following the track of the wild boar until the sun was low in the sky.
And so he passed the winter's day in this fashion
while his good guest was lying in bed beneath the blankets;
Sir Gawain stayed at home. In rich and deeply coloured garments
the lady didn't waste time
in greeting her true knight,
she went to him early

To greet her knight so true,
Early she took her way
To test his mood anew.

XIV

She to the curtain comes, and looks upon the knight,
Gawain doth greet her there in fitting wise and right;
She greeteth him again, ready of speech is she,
Soft seats her at his side, and laughs full merrily.
Then, with a smiling glance these words to him doth say:
"Sir, an ye be Gawain I marvel much alway,
So stern ye be when one would goodly ye entreat,
Of courteous company ignore the customs meet,
An one be fain to teach, swift from your mind they're brought
Since all forgotten now what yesterday I taught
By truest tokens all, that well might be, I trow."
"What is that?" quoth Gawain, "naught I remember now,
But if 't is sooth ye speak, then blame I needs must bear."
"Of kissing was my rede"; so quoth the lady fair,
"When countenance be known, swiftly a kiss to claim,
That doth become a knight who beareth courteous name!"
"Nay, cease, my dear, such speech," so quoth the gallant knight,
"A kiss I dare not claim, lest ye deny my right,
For an ye did forbid, to take, I trow, were wrong-
"I' faith," in merry wise she spake, "ye be too strong,
Ye may not be forbid, since ye may take with might
An any do such wrong as to deny thy right!"
"Yea," quoth Gawain, "by Christ, your speech it soundeth well,
But threats shall little thrive in that land where I dwell,

to test him out again.

She came to the curtains and looked at the knight,
and Gawain greeted her in the proper manner;
she greeted him again, quick to talk,
she sat softly at his side and laughed merrily.
Then she glanced at him, smiling, and said:
"Sir, it amazes me that you are Gawain,
you are so stern to one who makes requests of you,
and you ignore all the customs of courtly society,
and when someone tries to teach them, you forget them,
you don't remember what I told you yesterday
in the very plainest way possible."
"What is that?" asked Gawain, "I don't remember anything,
but if what you say is true then I am to blame."
"I told you about kissing," said the fair lady,
"that when you like a face you should claim a kiss at once,
that's what a chivalrous knight should do!"
"No, my dear, don't say that," said the gallant knight,
"I do not claim a kiss from you in case you deny me,
for it would be wrong to take one if you forbid it."
"I swear," she said in her merry way, "you are too strong,
you cannot be refused, since you could take kisses by force
from anyone who was wrong enough to refuse!"
"Yes," said Gawain, "by Christ, what you say sounds good,
but threats are not respected where I come from,
and we don't like things that are not offered freely;
I am at your command, to kiss, if that's what you want–take it or leave it, as you wish."
That fair lady bent with grace

64

Nor count we fair a gift that is not proffered free-
I am at your command, to kiss, if so shall be
Your will-to take or leave, as seemeth good to ye."
With grace,
She bent, that lady fair,
And gently kissed his face.
They hold sweet converse there,
Of love-themes speak a space.

and gently kissed his face.
Then they had a sweet talk
speaking of the things of love.

XV

"Fain would I ask of ye, (that lady questioned free)
If so ye were not wroth, what may the reason be
That one so young and fair, as ye be at this tide,
For knightly courtesie renowned both far and wide,
Who of all chivalry the head and chief men hold,
Versed in the lore of love, and warfare, fierce and bold-
Since each true knight doth tell how he did venture dare
(This token and this sign his deeds perforce must bear)
How for a lady's love his life at stake he set,
And for her favour fair full doleful dints hath met,
With valour 'venged her wrongs, and cured her of her care
Brought bliss unto her bower, and did her bounties share-
And ye be comeliest knight of this, your land and time,
Your worship and your words be famed in every clime,
And I, two mornings long have sat beside ye here
Yet never from your mouth a word came to mine ear
That ever dealt with love, in measure less or more;
But ye, so courteous held, so skilled in all such lore,
Surely to one so young as I should swiftly shew

"I would like to ask you," (the lady freely questioned),
"if it wouldn't offend you, why you,
who are so young and handsome as you are at this time,
known far and wide for knightly courtesy,
whom everyone holds up as the examplar of chivalry,
well versed in love, fierce and brave in war–
since every true knight says how he has adventured
(this is what people will call his deeds),
how he risked his life for the love of a lady,
and took terrible wounds to gain her favour,
revenged her wrongs with his bravery, and took away her cares,
brought happiness to her home, and partook of her goodness–
and you are the most handsome knight of this land and yours and this time,
your piety and your words are famous throughout the world,
and I have sat beside you here for two long mornings,
and have never heard a word from you dealing with love, great or small;
but you who are thought so courteous, so skilled in such matters,
should surely show one as young as I
some sign by which I could know true love.
Are you ignorant then, the one men praise so highly?
Or am I too dull for love, in your eyes?
It's a shame! I come and sit here

And teach some token sure, whereby true love
to know.
Are ye unlearn'd then, whom men so highly
prize?
Or am I all too dull for dalliance, in your eyes?
For shame!
Hither I come and sit
To learn, as at this same;
So teach me of your wit,
While sport my lord doth claim!"

to learn of this business;
so teach me what you know,
while my lord is hunting!"

XVI

"In good faith," quoth Gawain, "your good
deeds God repay,
For goodly is my glee, my profit great alway;
That one so fair as ye doth deign betake ye here
To please so poor a man, and me, your knight,
to cheer
With kindly countenance, in sooth doth please
me well
But that I, in my turn, should here of true love
tell,
And take that for my theme, (or tales of gallant
knight)
And teach ye, who I wot, doth wield more
skilful sleight
In such arts by the half, or hundred-fold indeed,
Than I, long as I live on earth may win for
meed,
'T were folly all indeed, sweet lady, by my fay!
Your will in troth I'll work in such wise as I
may,
As duteous I am bound-and ever more will do
Your service faithfully, God grant me grace
thereto!"
Thus did she ask him fair, and oft did test and
try,
To win him here to woo, whate'er her will
thereby-
But he doth fend him fair, nor ill hath done, I
ween,
And never deed of wrong hath chanced the
twain between,
but bliss-
They laugh and talk amain,
At last she doth him kiss,

"I swear," said Gawain, "God will repay you
for your good deeds,
for you bring me great happiness, you're good
for me;
it's wonderful that one so beautiful should
condescend
to please such a poor man and to bring
happiness to me, your knight,
with your sweet face, it really does give me
great pleasure.
But for me in exchange to tell you about true
love,
and make that my subject (or tales of gallant
knights)
and teach you, whom I'm sure is twice as skilful
in those
matters as I am, or indeed a hundred times
more,
than I am or ever will be, however long I live on
earth,
that would be true foolishness, sweet lady, I
swear!
I'll do whatever you want, as far as I can,
as I am duty-bound to do–and always will do–
your service faithfully, by the grace of God!"
So she asked him sweetly, testing him,
trying to get him to woo her, to do as she
wished–
but he defended himself skilfully, and did no
harm,
and nothing improper happened between them,
they were happy;
they laughed and talked a long time,
and at last she kissed him

Her leave of him hath ta'en,
And gone her way, I wis.

XVII

Then doth Sir Gawain rise, and robe him, mass
to hear.
Then was the dinner dight, and served with
mickle cheer;
Thus, with the ladies twain, in sport the day he
spent,
The while the lord doth chase the boar o'er bank
and bent-
Follows the grisly swine, as o'er the holts it
sped,
With broken back, his hounds, beneath its jaws
fall dead.
The boar would bide at bay, the bowmen grant
no grace,
But force him 'gainst his will once more his foes
to face.
So fast the arrows fly, the folk they gather
round,
Yet huntsmen stiff and stern, he startles at that
stound.
Till spent with flight, at last, he may no further
win,
But hies him in all haste, until a hole within
A mound, beside a rock, hard by the brooklet's
flow,
He gains-then turns at bay, tearing the ground
below.
His jaws, they foam and froth, unseemly to
behold,
He whets his tusks so white-was never man so
bold
Of those who faced him there, who dare the
issue try;
They eye him from afar, but none will venture
nigh.
Right wroth,
Many he smote before,
Thus all might well be loath
To face the tusks that tore-
So mad was he, i' troth.

and took her leave of him,
going on her way.

Then Sir Gawain rose and dressed to go to
Mass.
Then dinner was served, with much good cheer;
so he spent the day enjoying himself with the
two ladies,
while the lord chased the boar across the
country;
he followed the grim swine as it sped over the
hills,
breaking the backs of his hounds which fell dead
from its jaws.
When the boar tried to stand still the bowmen
wouldn't let him,
but forced him against his will to face his
enemies again.
The arrows flew so fast, the people gathered
round,
but even the bravest of the huntsmen was wary
of him.
But at last he was exhausted and could go no
further,
but got himself into a hole in a cliff, next to a
rock,
then turned at bay, pawing at the ground.
His jaws were horrid, covered in foam and
froth,
he sharpened his white tusks and the bravest
man of
all those who faced him dared not take him on;
they watched him from a distance, but none
would come close.
Furious, he had knocked down many already,
so that anyone might be afraid
to face his slashing tusks–
he really was so enraged.

XVIII

Then cometh swift the lord, spurring his goodly steed,
See'th the boar at bay, of his men taketh heed;
He lighteth from his horse, leaves it with hanging rein,
Draws out his blade so bright, and strideth forth amain.
Fast does he ford the stream, the boar bides on the strand,
"Ware of the gallant wight, with weapon fast in hand;
His bristles rise amain, grim were his snarls withal,
The folk were sore afraid, lest harm their lord befall.
The swine, with spring so swift, upon the hero fell,
That boar and baron bold none might asunder tell,
There, in the water deep, the boar, he had the worst,
For the man marked him well, e'en as they met at first,
His sharp blade in the slot he set, e'en to the heft,
And, driving hard and true, the heart asunder cleft,
Snarling, he yields his hold, the stream him hence hath reft.
Forthright,
The hounds, with fierce onslaught
Fall to, the boar they bite,
Swift to the shore he's brought,
And dogs to death him dight.

XIX

Forthwith from many a horn a joyful blast they blow,
Huntsmen together vie, high rings the loud "Hallo!"
The brachets bay their best, e'en at their masters' will,
Who in that fearsome chace had proved their hunters' skill.
And then a wight so wise in woodcraft, fit and fair,

Then the lord came hurrying, spurring on his good horse,
saw that the boar was cornered, saw what his men were doing;
he jumped from his horse, leaving the reins hanging,
drew out his bright sword and strode straight towards it.
He quickly crossed the stream, the boar waited on the bank,
wary of that gallant man holding his weapon tight;
all his bristles rose, and he gave grim snarls,
and the people were most afraid that their lord would come to harm.
The swine leapt at the hero so swiftly
and none could tell the boar and the Baron apart;
there, in the deep water, the boar got the worst of it,
for the man had deeply wounded him in their first clash,
he had got his sharp blade in the killing place up to the hilt,
and, driving hard and true, he split his heart apart,
so snarling, he relinquished his grip, and stumbled into the stream;
at once the hounds made a fierce attack,
leaping on, biting the boar,
quickly dragging him to the shore,
and the dogs did him to death.

Then many horns blew a joyful blast,
the huntsmen competing with each other in giving loud halloos.
The dogs copied their masters, barking as loudly,
the masters who had proved their skill as hunters in that wild chase.
And then a strong and handsome man, skilled in woodcraft,
set himself at once to skin the quarry.

The quarry to unlace hath set him straightway there.
He heweth off the head, and setteth it on high,
With skill he rendeth down the backbone, presently,
Then, bringing forth the bowels, roasts them on embers red,
And, to reward his hounds, doth blend them with their bread.
He strippeth off the brawn, e'en as in shields it were,
The hastlets hath he ta'en, and drawn them forth with care.
The halves he taketh now, and binds them as a whole,
With withy stiff and stout, made fast unto a pole.
And with that self-same swine homeward they fare thro' land;
The boar's head do they bear before their lord, on brand,
Who slew him in the ford, by force of his right hand
so strong-
Till he might see Gawain
In hall, he deemed it long,
His guest he was full fain
To pay, nor do him wrong.

He chopped off the head, and put it up high on a pole,
he skilfully slit down the backbone at once,
then he brought out the bowels, roasted them over a fire,
and to reward his hounds he mixed them with their bread.
He stripped off the flesh in chunks,
and drew out the innards carefully.
Then he took the two halves and tied them together
with stiff twine, attached to a pole,
and with that swine they journeyed home through the country;
they carried the boar's head in front of their lord on a stake,
the one who killed him in the ford with his strong right hand,
he was impatient to see Gawain,
it seemed ages until they got to the hall,
he was very keen to pay
his guest, not to cheat him.

XX

The lord, with merry jest, and laugh of gladsome glee
Soon as he saw Gawain, spake words both fair and free,
(The ladies too he bade, e'en with the household all-)
The boar's shields doth he show, and tells his tale withal,
How broad he was, how long, how savage in his mood,
That grisly swine-and how they chased him thro' the wood,
Sir Gawain doth commend his deeds, in comely wise,
Well hath he proved himself, to win so fair a prize-

The lord, with merry words and a happy laugh,
spoke sweetly and generously as soon as he saw Gawain
(he called the ladies too, and all the rest of the household),
he showed them the boar's flesh, and told his tale,
of how tall and broad he was, how savage,
that terrible swine, and how they chased him through the wood;
he warmly praised the deeds of Sir Gawain,
saying that he deserved such a fine prize,
"For such a strong beast," said the bold baron,
and such pigmeat, I have never seen before."
They handled the huge head, the knight gave it great praise,

"For such a brawny beast, (so spake that baron bold)
And such shields of a swine, mine eyes did ne'er behold."
They handle the huge head, the knight doth praise it well,
And loud and fair his speech, his host his mind may tell.
"Gawain," quoth the good man, "this gain is sure your own,
By forward fair and fast, e'en as before was shown."
"Yea," quoth the knight, "'t is true, and here too, by my troth,
I give ye all my gain, nor thereto am I loth."
With that he clasped his host, and doth him kindly kiss,
And so a second time he did the same, I wis.
"Now are we," quoth Gawain, "quit in this eventide
Of forwards all we made since I with ye abide in hall."
The lord quoth: "By Saint Giles,
I hold ye best withal,
Rich are ye in short, while
Your profits be not small!"

and he let his host know what he thought with loud acclamation.
"Gawain," said the good man, "this prize is surely yours,
sticking to the contract, as we did before."
"Yes," said the knight, "it's true, and I shall also keep my promise,
and give you everything I got, and I'm quite willing to."
With that he embraced his host, and sweetly kissed him,
and then did so again.
"Now we are," said Gawain, "even in this evening,
I have given you everything I've gained since I've been in your hall."
The lord said: "By St Giles,
I think you're doing well,
you'll soon be rich,
doing business like this!"

XXI

The tables then they bring, on trestles set aloft,
And cover them as meet, with cloths both fair and soft,
Clear falleth on the walls, of waxen torch, the light;
Sithen, to service fair they set them, many a knight.
Then clamour glad, and glee, arose within the hall,
Where flares the flame on floor they make much mirth withal,
They sing, e'en as they sup, and after, knights so true,
Fair songs of Christmas-tide, and many a carol new,
With every kind of mirth that man to tell were fain-
And by that lady's side he sat, the good Gawain,

Then they brought the tables, set up on trestles,
properly covered with fair soft cloths,
and the light of the wax candles reflected clearly off the walls;
then many knights began to enjoy their meals.
Then glad noises and merriment rose within the hall,
and there was much revelry around the hearth:
they sang even as they ate, and afterwards, those good knights,
sweet Christmas songs, and many new carols,
and they exchanged every kind of merry jest:
the good Gawain sat by the lady's side,
she looked so beautiful, so wise and demure,
and she pleased the gentle knight with sweet secret glances,
and he was much moved, and criticised himself,
but, out of honour, he would not look back,

Such semblance fair she made, in seemly wise and meet,
To please the gentle knight, with stolen glances sweet,
Whereat he marvelled much, and chid himself amain,
Yet, for his courtesy, would answer not again,
Dealing in dainty wise, till fate the die was fain to cast.
Thus made they mirth in hall,
Long as their will did last,
Then, when the lord did call,
To chimney-corner passed.

XXII

They drank, and dallied, there, and deemed 't were well to hold
Their forward fast and fair till New Year's Eve were told,
But Gawain prayed his leave, with morrow's morn to ride,
Since it were nigh the term his challenge to abide.
The lord withheld his leave, praying him strait to stay:
"As I be faithful knight, I pledge my troth alway
Thou shalt thy tryst fulfil, there at the Chapel Green,
Before the New Year's Morn hath waxed to prime, I ween;
So lie, and rest thee soft, and take thine ease at will,
And I shall hunt the holts, and keep our forward still,
To change my gain with thee, all that I homeward bear-
Twice have I tested thee, and found thee true and fair,
A third time will we try our luck, at dawn of day;
Now think ye upon joy, be merry while ye may,
For men may laugh at loss, if so their will alway."
Gawain doth grant the grace, and saith, he will abide;
Blithely they brought him drink, and then to bed

he would be cautious until fate decided matters.
So they celebrated in the hall,
as long as they had the energy,
then, when their lord called,
they went to the chimney breast.

They drank and chatted there and thought it would be good to keep
their bargain with each other until New Year's Eve was over,
but Gawain asked permission to ride the next morning,
since it was almost time to fulfil his challenge.
The lord would not give permission, urging him to stay:
"As I am a true knight, I give you my word
that you shall keep your appointment at the Green Chapel
before the morning of New Year's Day is up;
so sleep and get good rest, enjoy yourself,
and I shall hunt the foxes, and keep our bargain,
to exchange everything I bring home with you–
I have tried you twice, and found you fair and honest,
we'll try our luck a third time, at dawn;
now think of good things, be happy while you can,
for men can laugh at adversity, if their minds are right."
Gawain granted his request and said he would do as he asked;
then they merrily brought him drink, and then they went to bed by candlelight;
Sir Gawain lay and slept
softly through the quiet night,
and the lord kept his bargain,
for the hunt was arranged early.

they hied
with light-
Sir Gawain lies and sleeps
Soft, thro' the stilly night,
The lord his cov'nant keeps,
For chase is early dight.

XXIII

A morsel after mass, he taketh with his men,
Merry the morning tide-his mount he prayeth then,
They who, a-horse, should hold him company that day
A-saddle all, their steeds before the hall-gate stay.
Full fair it was a-field, the frost yet fast doth cling,
Ruddy, and red, the sun its rising beams doth fling,
And clear, and cloudless all, appears the welkin wide-
The huntsmen scatter them hard by a woodland side,
The rocks, they rang again before the horn's loud blast,
Some fell upon a track, where late a fox had passed-
(The trail may oft betray, tho' fox no feint doth lack-)
A hound hath found the scent, the hunt is on his track,
The dogs, they follow fast, and thick the hue and cry,
They run in rabble rout on the trail speedily
The fox, he fled apace, the hounds their prey have seen,
And, once within their sight, they follow fast and keen,
Loudly they threaten there, with cry and clamour fierce
The fox, with twist and turn, the undergrowth doth pierce,
Winding, and hearkening oft, low thro' the hedge doth creep,
Then, by a little ditch, doth o'er a spinney leap,
So, still, he stealeth forth, by rough and rugged

He ate a snack after mass with his men,
it was a fine morning and he called for his horse;
those who would come with him that day were already
mounted at the gates of the castle.
The fields were beautiful, the frost still covering them,
and the sun, red as it rose, threw out its beams,
and there wasn't a cloud in the whole of the sky.
The huntsmen scattered around the edge of the wood,
and the rocks once again rang to the loud blast of the horn.
Some found a track where a fox had recently passed
(the trail can often give them away, though the fox does not lack cunning)
the hounds found the scent, and the hunt got on his track,
the dogs followed quickly and there was a great commotion;
they ran pell-mell along the trail,
the fox ran fast, but the hounds had seen their prey,
and once it was in view they followed fast and keen,
making loud threats, with a great fierce racket,
while the fox twisted and turned, slipping into the undergrowth,
twisting and always listening, he crept low through the hedge,
then, by a little ditch, he leapt into a spinney,
so he quietly sneaked along, on a rough and rugged path,
hoping to escape the wood and cheat the hounds that day;
then, before he knew what was happening, he'd

way
Thinking to clear the wood, and cheat the hounds that day;
Then, ere he wist, I trow, to hunters' tryst he came
Threatened he was threefold, by hounds as at that same:
from fray
He starteth swift aside,
And fled, as he were fey;
Fain was he at that tide
To seek the woodland way.

come across the hunters,
so he was attacked from three sides, by the hounds as well:
he dodged quickly aside
and fled, terrified;
at that time he wanted
to find his way through the woods.

XXIV

'T was lively then to list the hounds, as loud they cry,
When all the pack had met, and mingled, speedily,
Such wrath, methinks, adown upon his head they call
As all the climbing cliffs had clashed unto their fall.
Hunters, with loud "Halloo," sight of their prey do hail,
Loudly they chide the fox, nor scolding speech doth fail,
Threaten him once and oft, and "thief" they call him there-
The hounds are on his trail, tarry he may not dare,
Oft would they him out-run, and head him ere he passed,
Double again he must-wily the fox, and fast,
Thus, by his skill he led master and huntsmen bold
O'er hill, o'er dale, by mount, by woodland, and by wold;
While the good knight at home doth soundly sleep, I ween,
All comely curtained round, on morning cold and keen.
But Love the lady fair had suffered not to sleep,
That purpose to impair which she in heart doth keep.
Quickly she rose her up, and thither took her way

It was thrilling then to hear the hounds as they barked loudly,
when all the pack came together and joined,
they brought such noise down upon his head
it was as if the cliff was falling upon him.
The hunters, with a loud "Halloo!" greeted the sight of their prey,
and they loudly abused the fox, they didn't let up on him,
they threatened him over and over, and called him "thief";
the hounds were on his trail, he didn't dare to wait,
often they would outrun him, and head him off before he passed,
so that he had to double back; the fox was cunning, and fast,
and so by his skill he led the master and his bold huntsmen
over hills and dales, peaks, woodland and fields;
while the good knight was sleeping soundly at home,
inside his comfortable curtains, on a cold sharp morning.
But love had not allowed the fair lady to sleep,
and she had not lost sight of her heart's desire.
She quickly got up and made her way
wrapped in a fine cloak, which swept along the ground.
Inside it was richly lined with fur, and had fur trimmings,

In mantle meet enwrapped, which swept the ground alway.
Within, 't was finely furred, and bordered with the same,
No gold doth bind her head but precious stones, aflame,
Within her tresses wound, by twenties cluster fair;
Her face, and eke her throat, the mantle leaveth bare,
Bare is her snow-white breast, and bare her back to sight;
Passing the chamber door, she shuts it close and tight-
Setting the window wide, she calls her knight alway,
And, laughing, chideth him in merry words and gay,
With cheer,
"Ah, man! Why dost thou sleep?
The morn dawns fair and clear,"
Gawain, in slumber deep,
Dreaming, her voice did hear.

XXV

Drowsing, he dreamed, the knight, a dream with travail fraught,
As men, in morning hours, are plagued with troubled thought;
How destiny, next morn, his weird should duly dight,
When, at the Chapel Green, he needs must meet that knight,
And there his buffet bide, nor make there for debate-
But, came that comely dame, his wits he summoned straight,
Aroused him from his sleep, and spake full speedily;
That lady drew anigh, sweet was her smile to see-
She bent her o'er his face, and kissed him, fair and free.
A greeting fit he gave, in words of gladsome cheer,
So glorious her guise, clad in such goodly gear,

she had no gold around her head but gleaming precious stones
were wound within her hair, in many lovely groups;
the cloak left her face and her throat bare,
and her snowwhite breast and her back were bare to sight;
passing the chamber door, she closed it up tight,
she threw the window open wide and called to her knight,
and, laughing, mocked him with merry cheerful words:
"Ah, man! Why are you sleeping?
The morning has come, fair and clear."
Gawain, sleeping deeply,
dreamt that he could hear her voice.

He dreamed as he slept, the knight, a terrible dream,
for men are cursed with troubled thoughts in the morning,
of how the next morning fate would decide his destiny,
when he had to meet the knight at the Green Chapel,
and endure the blow without argument;
but when that sweet lady came, he gathered his wits together,
awoke from his sleep, and spoke at once;
the lady came near, her smile was sweet to see;
she bent over his face, and kissed him, sweetly and openly.
He gave her a proper greeting, with words of happiness,
she looked so beautiful, clad in such fine clothes,
her features all faultless, her colour wonderful,
that the springs of joy overflowed, his heart was

Her features faultless all, her colour fair and fine,
The springs of joy well free, warming his heart like wine;
Their seemly smiles full swift were smitten into mirth,
Bliss, and good fellowship, betwixt the twain to birth
did win-
Their words were fair and good,
Weal reigned those walls within,
Yet peril 'twixt them stood,
Nor might she nearer win.

XXVI

She pressed that prince of price so close, I trow, that day,
Leaning so nigh her point, that need upon him lay
To take her proffered love, or roughly say her nay-
For courtesy his care, lest he be craven knight,
And more, lest mischief fall, in that he sin outright,
And thus betray his host, the lord of house and hall,
"God shield me," quoth the knight, "that e'er such chance befall!"
Forthwith, with laughter light, he strove to lay aside
All speech of special grace her lips might speak that tide;
Then quoth she to the knight: "I hold ye worthy blame
An ye love not that life which here your love doth claim,
And lieth wounded here, above all else on earth,
Save ye a true love have ye hold of better worth,
And to that lady fair your faith so fast ye hold,
Ye may not list my words-Save ye that tale have told
That will I not believe-I pray ye, of a sooth,
For all the love on life, hide not from me the truth
for guile?"
The knight quoth: "By Saint John,

warmed as by wine;
their pleasant smiles soon turned to laughter,
happiness and friendship arose between the two;
their words were sweet and good,
there was much happiness there;
but it was a dangerous situation,
if Gawain was not careful.

She pushed that fine prince so far that day,
getting so near her goal, that he had to
either take the love she offered, or roughly
reject her;
he wanted to be a good knight and not show any
rudeness,
but even more importantly he wanted to avoid
sinning,
and so betray his host, the lord of the castle.
"God protect me," said the knight, "against that
ever happening!"
And so with light jokes he tried to deflect
any especially affectionate speech she made that
morning;
then she said to the knight: "I am not happy
with you,
you don't love the life of the one whose love you
claim,
who is wounded here, above anything else on
earth,
you must have a love that you value more,
and you are keeping faith with that fair Lady,
so you don't listen to me–you have told a tale
that I will not believe–I ask you, truthfully,
for all the love in the world, are you not hiding
the truth from me?"
The knight said: "By St John,"
(and he smiled gaily)
I have no true love,
nor will I have, for a while!"

(And gaily did he smile)
Of true love have I none,
Nor will I, for a while!"

XXVII

"That word," the lady quoth, "methinks hath grieved me more,
Yet I my answer take, altho' I sorrow sore;
But kiss me kindly now, ere yet I go my way
My fate to mourn on mould, as she who loveth may."
Sighing, she swayed adown, and kissed the knight so good,
Then raised her up again, and spake e'en as she stood:
"At this our parting, dear, grant me this grace for love,
Give me somewhat as gift, if it be but thy glove,
That I may think on thee, and so my grief may still
"Now, I wis," quoth the knight, "I would I had at will,
The thing I hold on earth most precious, it were thine,
Ye have deserved, I trow, by friendship fair and fine,
A guerdon goodlier far than I might e'er bestow!
But here, by gift of love, small profit might ye know,
Nor were ye honoured now, had ye at this time aught
Or glove, or other gift, from Gawain, as ye sought;
Here thro' the land I fare on errand strange and dread,
No men have I with mails, or trinkets, at this stead,
That much misliketh me, lady, for this thy sake,
Yet, be 't for good or ill, each man his chance must take
aright-"
"Thou knight of honour, nay"
(So spake the lady bright),
"Tho' no gift be my pay
Somewhat I'll give my knight."

"That word," the lady said, "has upset me even more,
but I'll take that as your answer, although it grieves me;
but kiss me sweetly now, before I go away,
to bemoan my fate on earth, as lovers do."
Sighing, she bent down, and kissed that good knight,
then stood up again, and spoke as she stood:
"As we part, dear, do me this favour for love,
give me something as a gift, if it's only your glove,
so I can think of you, and calm my grief."
"Now I swear," said the knight, "I wish I had at my command
the most precious thing to me on earth, it would be yours,
you have deserved, I swear, for your good and sweet friendship,
a token far better than anything I can give!
You would have a great gift if at any other time
you had asked for a glove or something else from Gawain;
but travelling through this land I am on a strange and deadly errand,
and I don't have men carrying my luggage or trinkets with me,
and that upsets me, lady, for this reason,
but for better or worse everyone must take his chances-"
"You honourable knight, no,"
said the fair lady,
"although I get no gift from you,
I'll give something to my knight."

XXVIII

She proffered him a ring, of red gold fashioned fair,
A sparkling stone, I trow, aloft the setting bare,
Its gleam, in sooth, outshone the sunlight's ruddy ray,
I wot well that its worth no man might lightly pay.
Gawain the ring refused, and readily he spake:
"No gift, my lady gay, of goodwill will I take,
Since I have naught to give naught will I take of thee-"
Straitly she prayed, Gawain refused her steadfastly,
Sware swiftly on his sooth, that ring he would not take-
The lady, sorely grieved, in this wise further spake:
"An ye refuse my ring, methinks, the cause shall be
Ye deem ye were too much beholden unto me,
I'll here my girdle give as lesser gift this tide-"
She loosed a silken lace that hung low at her side,
Upon her kirtle knit, beneath her mantle's fold,
With green silk was it gay, entwined with threads of gold,
Braided in cunning wise, by skilful fingers wrought;
She proffered it the knight, and blithely him besought
To take this as her gift, tho' worthless all it were-
But still he said her nay, and, ever steadfast, sware
He would nor gift nor gold, ere God would give him grace
Well to achieve the chance t'wards which he set his face-
"Therefore, I pray ye now, be not displeased at this,
But let the matter be, I may not grant, I wis, thy prayer
Much do I owe to thee
For this, thy gentle care,
By heat, by cold, I'll be

She offered him a ring, beautifully made of red gold,
the sparkling stones standing out from the setting,
its gleam outshining the red rays of the sun,
I'm sure it was a very expensive thing.
Gawain refused the ring, and quickly spoke:
"My sweet lady, I cannot accept any gift from you,
as I have nothing to give I won't take anything."
She implored him again, but Gawain steadfastly refused,
swearing upon his honour that he would not take the ring;
the lady, greatly upset, spoke further:
"If you refuse my ring, I think the reason is you don't want to be in debt to me,
so I'll give you my girdle as a small gift."
She undid a silk belt that hung low at her side,
hanging round her dress, beneath her cloak,
it was of bright green silk, embroidered with golden threads,
cunningly woven by skilful hands;
she offered it to the knight, and sweetly asked him
to take this as a gift, although it was worthless.
But still he refused her, and, resolute, swore
he wouldn't take presents or money, before God in his grace allowed him
to complete the quest he had set himself:
"So, please, don't be upset by this,
but leave it, I can't grant your request;
I owe much to you,
for your kind care of me,
in all weathers I'll be
your servant everywhere."

Thy servant everywhere."

XXIX

"Do ye refuse this silk," so quoth the gentle dame,
"For its simplicity? I grant ye of that same;
Lo! light it is to hold, and less its cost, I ween,
Yet who the virtue knew that knit therein hath been,
Would peradventure prize it higher for its grace-
Whoso shall gird himself with this same woven lace
The while 't is knotted well around him, 't is a charm,
And no man upon mould may wreak him hurt or harm,
And ne'er may he be slain by magic, or by spell-"
Sir Gawain, in his heart, that hour bethought him well,
That lace a jewel were against the jeopardy
Which, at the Chapel Green, did wait him presently,
Might he escape un-slain, the sleight he deemed were good;
Thus suffered he her prayer, and shewed a gentler mood.
She pressed on him her gift, and urged him loud and still,
He granted her the grace, she gave it of good will,
And, for her sake, besought he tell the matter ne'er,
But hide it from her lord, he sware it fast and fair,
That no man, save them twain, should this, their secret, share
for naught-
He thanked her oft, I wis,
joyful of heart and thought,
Her true knight did she kiss
Thrice, ere she leave besought.

"Do you refuse this silk," asked the sweet lady,
"because it's too simple? I know that you're right;
it doesn't weigh very much, and it cost less,
but someone who knew the power that was woven into it,
would perhaps set a higher value upon it:
whoever wears this woven lace,
while it is tied around him, it is a charm,
and no man on earth can cause him any harm,
and he can never be killed by magic or by spells."
Sir Gawain, in his heart, thought it was his lucky day,
and that lace would be a charm against the danger
which he would soon face at the Green Chapel;
if he could escape unharmed, he thought it would be a good trick;
so he listened to her prayer, and became more amenable.
She insisted he take her gift, urging him loudly and constantly,
and he did as she wanted, she gave it freely,
and begged him for her sake never to tell of it,
but hide it from her lord, and he swore
that no person, apart from them, would ever know their secret:
he gave her much thanks,
rejoicing in heart and mind,
she kissed her true knight
three times, before she asked to leave.

XXX

Then, laughing, saith, "Farewell," and from the room doth go

Then, laughing, she said, "Farewell," and left the room,

For more mirth of that man, I wot, she may not know;
When she hath gone, Gawain doth from his couch arise,
And swiftly robes himself in rich and royal wise,
Taketh the love-lace green, his lady's gift so fair,
That wound around his waist he doth well hidden bear.
Then to the chapel, swift, the knight doth take his way,
And, seeking out a priest, he privily doth pray
He may his life unfold, that he may better know
How his soul may be saved, when he from hence shall go.
Shrived was he surely there-he shewed his misdeeds all,
Or less they be or more, and did for mercy call,
Then, from the listening priest, doth absolution pray-
Assoil.d well he was, and set as clean alway
As if the morrow's morn the day of doom should be.
Sithen he makes good cheer amid the ladies free,
With comely carols there, all joys men may devise,
(As ne'er before that day, methinks, had been his wise)
with bliss-
That all men marvelled there
And said of him, I wis,
Such semblance gay he ware
As none had seen ere this.

XXXI

Now let him linger there where love his share shall be-
The lord is yet afield, leading his folk so free,
Now hath he slain the fox, that he hath chased all day-
As he thro' spinney sped, eager to spy his prey,
There, where he heard the hounds that close on his track lay,
Lo! Reynard, running low, thro' tangled grove

---

for that was all she was going to get from that man;
when she had gone, Gawain rose from his bed,
and swiftly dressed himself in rich and noble fashion,
taking the green lovelace, his lady's sweet gift,
and carried it wound round his waist, well hidden.
Then the knight swiftly made his way to the chapel,
and, finding a priest, he begged to be allowed to make his confession, so that he could know how his soul could be saved, when he left the Earth.
He certainly was forgiven there, he confessed all of his sins,
the greater and the lesser, and asked for mercy, and prayed for absolution from the listening priest;
he was completely cleansed, and sent away as stainless
as if tomorrow morning would be Judgement Day.
Then he enjoyed himself with the ladies, with sweet carols, all the happiness men can think of,
better than he had ever known before, I think;
and everyone marvelled at him,
and they all said of him
that he looked happier
than they had ever seen a man before.

Now let him rest there where he gets love;
the lord was still in the field, chasing after the fox,
which he had now killed, having chased it all day.
As he sped through the spinney, eager to see his prey,
there, where he heard the hounds that followed him closely,

he steals,
And all the yelping pack of hounds are at his heels.
The knight, he saw the beast, and would his coming wait,
Drew forth his brand so bright, and flung it swift and straight,
The fox, the sharp sword shunned, to swerve aside was fain,
A hound doth hold him fast ere he might turn again,
Beneath the horse's feet the pack upon him fell,
Worried their wily prey with many a yap and yell,
The lord, he lights adown, the fox he seizes there,
Swiftly he snatches him from out the jaws that tear,
Holding him high o'er head, he halloos loud and gay,
While many a gallant hound doth round him spring and bay.
Thither the huntsmen hie, their horns sound merrily,
Answering each to each, till all their master see.
That noble company, they gather fair and fast,
All who the bugle bare together blew a blast,
While they who had no horn, they halloo'd loud and clear;
It was the merriest meet that ever man might hear
The clamour that was raised o'er Reynard's doom so drear
Then, gay,
The hounds they there reward,
Rubbing their heads that day-
Now have they ta'en Reynard
And stript his pelt away.

XXXII

And then they hied them home, for night-fall was full nigh,
Blowing a shattering blast on horn, with notes so high,
The lord at last alights before his home so dear,
A fire he finds on floor-his guest, he sitteth near,

was the fox, running low through the tangled bushes,
with all the yelping pack of hounds on his heels.
The knight saw the beast and waited for him to arrive,
drew out his bright sword, and threw it swift and straight;
the fox tried to swerve to avoid the sharp sword,
and a hound grabbed him before he could turn back.
Under the horse's feet the pack fell on him,
shaking their cunning prey with many yaps and yelps.
The lord leapt down and grabbed the fox,
quickly snatching him away from the tearing jaws;
holding him high overhead he halloo'ed loud and happy,
while many brave hounds gambolled barking around him.
The huntsmen rushed there, blowing their merry horns,
calling each to each, until they could all see their master.
That noble company quickly came together,
and all who carried a horn joined in a great blast,
while those who had no horn gave a loud halloo;
it was the merriest noise that a man could hear,
that song that was sung over the dreadful fate of the fox;
then they happily rewarded their hounds,
stroking all their heads;
then they took the fox
and stripped off his pelt.

And then they headed home, for it was almost night,
blowing shattering blasts shrill on the horn,
and the lord at last dismounted at his dear home,
finding a fire on the hearth, with his guest sitting nearby,

Gawain the good, who glad and joyous was withal,
For, mid the ladies fair, bliss to his lot did fall.
He ware a robe of blue, e'en to the earth it fell,
His surcoat, softly furred, became him passing well;
Of self-same stuff, the hood upon his shoulders lay,
Bordered and bound the twain with fur alike that day.
His host he met forthwith, there, in the midmost hall,
A goodly greeting gave, and joyful spake withal;
"Now shall I first fulfil thy forward, mine and thine,
Which we together sware whenas ye spared no wine."
With that he clasped the knight, and gave him kisses three,
Setting them on his lips with all solemnity.
"By Christ," then quoth the host: "good fortune yours hath been,
If for such chance ye gave a fair exchange, I ween!"
"Thereof small need to speak-" the hero straightway said,
"Since light the cost, and swift, methinks, the price I paid."
"By Mary," quoth his host, "in that am I behind,
I hunted all this day, and yet I naught might find
Save this foul fox's pelt, fiend take the thing alway,
Methinks for precious gifts the same were sorry pay.
And ye have rendered me three kisses here to-day
right good-"
"Enough," quoth Sir Gawain,
"I thank ye, by the Rood."
Then how the fox was slain
He told him as they stood.

XXXIII

Of mirth, of minstrelsy, of meat, they take their fill,
And make them merry there, as men may do at

Gawain the good, who was glad and happy,
for he was having a wonderful time with the ladies.
He wore a blue robe which fell down to the earth,
and his topcoat, fur lined, suited him very well;
a hood made of the same stuff lay on his shoulders,
that day they were both lined and edged with fur.
He greeted his host at once, there in the middle of the hall,
gave him a warm welcome, and also spoke happily;
"Now I shall be the first to fulfil the promise, yours and mine,
which we swore together and sealed over a drink of wine."
With that he embraced the knight, and kissed him three times,
putting them on his lips solemnly.
"By Christ," the host then said, "you have had plenty of luck,
if you paid a fair price for these things you got, I think!"
"There is little need to speak of it," the hero said at once,
"since I have handed over everything I received."
"By Mary," said his host, "now I am in debt,
I hunted all day, and yet all I could find
was this foul fox's pelt, devil take it,
and I think it's a sorry exchange for such precious gifts.
And you have given me three fine kisses here today–"
"Enough," said Sir Gawain,
"I thank you, by the Holy Cross."
Then as they stood there he told him how the fox was killed.

They had their fill of music and food and fun,
and they were as merry as men can be when
they have the sweet laughter of ladies and merry

will,
With ladies' laughter light, and many a merry
jest,
So joyful were the twain, the host, and his good
guest,
E'en as they drunken were, or e'en had waxen
fey-
The lord, and e'en his men made many a jest so
gay,
Until at length the time for severance was o'er
past,
Each baron to his bed betook him at the last.
Then first, Sir Gawain good, leave of his host
would pray
Thanking him fair and free, and thus he spake
alway:
"For this fair sojourning your honour be
increased,
The High King grant ye this, I pray, at this high
feast.
Your servant here am I, an so your will may be-
With morn I needs must fare, e'en as I told to
ye,
A guide ye promised sure, to shew to me the
way
To that same Chapel Green, where, on the New
Year's Day
With God's will shall be dealt my doom, and
this, my weird-"
"In good faith," quoth the host, "be not for that
afeard,
Of good will shall I give all that to ye I hight-"
A servant then he called, to shew the way aright
Fair o'er the downs, that so Gawain should have
no need
To wend by words, but through the copse, might
make with speed
his way-
For gracious fare, Gawain,
With gracious words would pay,
And from the ladies twain
His leave was loth to pray.

XXXIV

Careful he kissed the twain, and spake them
both full fair,

jests,
the two were so happy, the host and his good
guest,
as if they were drunk, or had gone mad;
the lord and also his men made so many merry
jokes,
until it was past time for them to part,
and finally each baron went to his bed.
So first good Sir Gawain took leave of his host,
thanking him kindly and sweetly, saying to him:
"May you get the praise you deserve for your
kind hospitality,
I pray to God to grant to this, this Christmas time.
I am your servant, and I hope you will help me;
in the morning I must go, as I have told you,
to where you promised you would guide me,
to that Green Chapel, where, on New Year's
Day,
by God's will I shall face my fate, my doom."
"I swear," said the host, "you don't need to
worry about that,
I'll give you everything I said I would."
Then he called a servant, to show him the right
way,
straight over the downs, so that Gawain would
have no need
to ask the way, but might go straight through
the woods quickly:
Gawain repaid such sweet hospitality
with sweet words,
and he was very reluctant
to say farewell to the two ladies.

He sweetly kissed them both, and spoke to them
courteously,

Well may they thrive for thanks he presseth on them there.
And in the selfsame wise those ladies make reply,
Commending him to Christ, with many a piteous sigh.
Then from the household all, in courteous wise he 'ld part,
And each man that he met, he thanked him from his heart
For service, solace fair, and for the pains they knew
In that they busied them to do him service true.
And all to say "Farewell," I trow, such sorrow felt
As if in worthy wise long years with him they 'd dwelt.
With torches burning bright, they to his chamber led,
And, that he well might rest, blithely brought him to bed.
But that he soundly slept, in sooth, I dare not say,
Matter enow had he, that came with dawning day
for thought-
Now let him lie there still,
He nigheth what he sought-
If hearken me ye will
I'll tell ye how they wrought.

and they should prosper from the good wishes he offered them there.
The ladies answered in the same way,
asking Christ to protect him, with many sad sighs.
Then he said polite goodbyes to the whole household,
and every man he met, he thanked him from his heart
for his service, his fair comfort, and for the trouble they had taken
to serve him as well as they could.
And I believe that everyone felt such sorrow in saying farewell
that it was as if they had lived with him for many years.
With the torches burning bright, they led him to his room,
and brought him sweetly to his bed, so that he could rest.
But I can't truthfully say that he slept soundly,
for he had enough to think about the coming day;
and now he lay there still,
almost at the end of his quest;
if you listen to me
I'll tell you what happened.

Book Four

I

Now nigheth the New Year, past are the hours of night,
And, e'en as God doth will, darkness must yield to light,
But weather wild awakes e'en with the New Year's birth,
Aloft, the driving clouds cast the keen cold to earth,
Enow of North therein the naked wight to slay-
The snow, it smartly drave across the fells that day,
With whistling blast the wind doth whirl it from on high,
Till, in each dale, the drifts both wide and deep they lie.
The knight, he hearkened well, as in his bed he lay,
But, tho' his eyes were shut, little he slept alway.
By every cock that crew, the hour right well he knew,
And lightly gat him up, ere yet to dawn it drew,
For in the chamber burned a lamp that gave him light
His chamberlain he called, who answered him forthright,
Bade him his byrnie bring, and saddle his good steed;
The other gat him up, and swiftly fetched his weed,
Then was Sir Gawain clad in fitting wise, and fair,
First, in his clothes he 's wrapt, the cold from him to 'ware,
Then he his harness doffs, that well was kept, I ween,
The plates, the coat of mail, alike are polished clean,
And of his byrnie rich, the rings from rust are freed,
'T was fresh as at the first-Of thanks, he fain full meed
would bring-
He did on him each piece,
They lacked no burnishing,

Now the New Year had come, the night was over,
and as God has ordered, darkness gave way to light.
But the start of the New Year brought wild weather,
above the driving clouds brought freezing cold to earth,
northerly enough to kill an unprotected man;
the snow drove forward across the fells that day,
and the whistling wind drove it down from above,
until, in every valley, there were wide deep snow drifts.
The knight listened to this as he lay in bed,
and though his eyes were shut, he got little sleep.
He knew the time from the crowing of the cocks,
and quietly got up, before the dawn arrived,
for he had a lamp in the room to give him light.
He called his servant, who came at once,
and told him to bring his mail and saddle his horse;
the other got up and quickly fetched his clothes,
so Sir Gawain was dressed well and handsomely,
first he was wrapped in his clothes to keep him from the cold,
then he put on his armour, which had been well looked after,
the plates and mail coat were both well polished,
there was no rust on the rings of his chainmail,
it was good as new, and he gladly gave thanks for that;
he put on each piece,
they were all well polished,
the brightest in all the world,
and he told them to bring him his horse.

Gayest from here to Greece,
His steed he bade them bring.

II

The while in richest weed he doth himself array,
His coat, with cognizance embroidered clear and gay,
On velvet, rich adorned, with stones of virtue high
Well wrought and bound, the seams embroidered cunningly,
And all, with fairest skins, within well furred and lined-
The lace, the lady's gift, he doth not leave behind,
Gawain forgat it not, since 't was for his own good-
He belted fast his brand around him as he stood,
Then twined the token twice, and drew it round him tight,
Well did that silken cord enswathe the goodly knight;
The girdle of green silk, in sooth, beseemed him well,
On cloth of royal red, its hues, they richly tell.
But for that girdle's grace he ware it not, the knight,
Nor for the pendants' pride, tho' polished they, and bright,
Nor for the glittering gold, whose gleam the ends doth light-
But 't was to save himself, when he must shortly stand
And bide without debate, from knife or glittering brand
a blow-
Now, armed, the goodly knight
Forth from the hall doth go,
On all who there be dight
His thanks he would bestow.

*Then he dressed himself in the richest clothes,
his coat had his emblem embroidered clear and handsome,
on velvet, richly decorated, with valuable stones
well cut and sewn, with cunningly embroidered seams,
and all lined with the best furs.
He did not leave behind the lady's gift of lace,
Gawain had not forgotten it, since it was for his own good:
he tied his sword on fast as he stood there,
and then wrapped the token around him twice, tying it tight,
that silken band wrapped snugly around the gallant knight;
the belt of green silk truly suited him well,
showing up nicely against the deep red cloth.
But he wasn't wearing that belt for protection, the knight,
nor for the beauty of the decorations, though they were polished and bright,
nor for the glittering gold, which gleamed on the ends;
it was to save himself, when soon he would stand
and take a blow from a knife or a glittering sword without argument.
Now the good knight
went out from the hall,
giving his thanks
to everyone who was there.*

III

Ready was Gringalet, his charger great and tall,
Stabled the steed had been in fitting wise withal,
Eager to start, the horse delay might little brook-
The knight, he drew anear, and on his coat did

*Gringalet was ready, his great tall charger,
the horse had been very well looked after,
and was eager to start, it didn't want to waste time.*

look,
Spake softly to himself, and by his sooth he
sware,
"The men within this moat for honour fitly care,
May they, with their good lord, all joy
henceforward share,
And may love be her meed thro' life, that fair
ladie,
Who thus a passing guest cherish for charitie,
And honour hold in hand-may He repay withal
Who rules on high, the folk within this goodly
hall,
If I my life on land might somewhat longer lead
Then readily reward I 'ld give, as fits your meed
He to the stirrup steps, and doth his steed
bestride,
Upon his shoulder lays his shield as fit, that tide,
Then spurreth Gringalet, anon, with spurs of
gold,
The steed no longer stands, but on the stones so
cold
doth dance-
Mounted, his squire doth bear
Aloft, his spear and lance,-
"Christ keep this castle fair
And give it aye good chance."

IV

They let the bridge adown, the gateway, broad
and wide,
Unbar, and open set the door on either side;
The knight, he crossed himself, and passed the
castle bound,
Praising the porter good, who, kneeling low on
ground,
Gave him Good-day, and prayed that God might
save Gawain-
So doth he wend his way, with one wight in his
train,
To lead him to that place of peril stern and grim,
Where he must pay the price, where bale
awaiteth him.
By hedgerow winds their way, where boughs are
stripped and bare,
Anon, they climb the cliffs, where cold and chill
the air,

*When the knight came close he looked at his
coat,
and spoke softly to himself, and he swore,
"The men of this castle truly care for honour,
and may they and their good lord from now on
have all happiness,
and may that fair lady have love throughout her
life,
who was so sweet to a passing guest out of
kindness,
and treated him so honourably; may God
reward
the people in this fine castle.
If I am allowed to stay on earth a little longer
then I will gladly give you the reward you
deserve."
He stepped up to the stirrups, and mounted his
horse,
he slung his shield over his shoulder
then spurred on Gringalet with his golden spurs,
and the horse no longer stood, but danced on
the cold stones:
mounted, his master held
his spear and lance aloft, saying,
"May Christ keep this castle safe
and always give it his blessing."*

*They lowered the drawbridge and unlocked the
broad wide
gateway, and flung the doors open;
the knight crossed himself and left the precincts
of the castle,
praising the good porter, who knelt low on the
ground
and wished him good day, and prayed that God
might save Gawain.
So he went on his way, with one man with him,
to take him to that harsh grim place of danger
where he had to pay the price, where his fate
awaited.
They went along by a hedgerow, where the
branches were stripped and bare,
then soon they climbed the cliffs, where the air
was cold and chill,*

The heaven its showers up-held, but here on earth 't was ill,

In mist was merged the moor, mist clung to every hill,

Each ware a cap of cloud, and cloak of mist so dank;

Bubbling, the brooks they brake in foam upon the bank,

Splashed sheer upon the shores, there, where they shelved adown,

Yea, lone and drear the way, beneath the dark wood's frown

Until the rising sun with gold the hillcrest crown that tide-

They climbed a hill full high

White snow lay on its side,

The guide, who rode hard by,

Now bade him to abide.

V

"Now lord, as I was pledged, I have ye hither led,

Now are ye nigh the place of note, your quest is sped

That ye have straitly sought, and asked for specially,

But now I know ye well, in sooth, I'ld say to ye-

(Since ye be such a lord that men full well may love,)

Would ye but work my will your welfare it might prove

The place whereto ye pass right perilous men hold,

A wight doth ward that waste, the worst is he on mould,

For stiff is he, and stern, and over keen to strike,

For height on middle-earth no man hath seen his like;

Bigger of body he, than any four who won

A place in Arthur's house, yea, e'en were Hector one!

And this his custom cursed-here at the Chapel Green

There passeth never man, tho' proud in arms, I ween,

But he doth do to death by dint of deadly blow,

Heaven held back its showers, but on the Earth it was grim,
the moors were covered in mist, there was fog on every hill,
each one had a cap of cloud, and a cloak of dank mist;
the streams rushed foaming through their banks,
splashing on the shores where they fell down in waterfalls.
It was a lonely and miserable journey, beneath the frowning dark woods,
until the rising sun capped the hilltops with gold:
they climbed a great high hill,
with white snow on its sides:
the guide, riding close by,
now told him to wait.

Now lord, as I have promised, I have brought you here,
you are close to the place you're looking for, you have found
that which you looked for, and asked for specially,
but now I know you well, I shall say to you
(since you are a lord whom men can easily revere)
that if you just do what I suggest it will be good for you.
The place to which you're going is known to be dangerous,
the man who rules that region is the worst man on earth,
he is strong and stern and too quick to strike,
and nobody has ever seen a taller man on earth;
his body is larger than any four of Arthur's knights together, even if Hector were one of them!
And it is his cursed custom here at the Green Chapel
that no man ever passes, however fine a fighter,
without him killing him with a deadly blow,
for he has no chivalry, and does not know mercy.

For all discourteous he, nor mercy doth he know.
Chaplain be he, or churl, who by that chapel rides,
Mass priest, or hooded monk, or any man beside,
Is he as fain to slay as he himself to live-
So soothly as ye sit on steed, this rede I give:
Go ye there, with his will, ye come not hence alive-
Trow me, I speak the truth-yea, had ye twenty lives
to spend-
Long time hath he dwelt here,
His conquests know no end,
Against his dints so drear
No shield may ye defend.

If a chaplain or peasant rides past that Chapel,
a priest or a hooded monk, any sort of man,
he would give his life to kill them;
so as you sit here on your horse, I give you this advice:
if you go there at his order you will not come out alive,
believe me, I speak the truth, even if you had twenty lives to spend:
he has lived there a long time,
he has never been beaten,
there is no shield which could defend
against his terrible blows.

VI

"Wherefore, Sir Gawain good, let ye this man alone,
And for God's sake, I pray, from this place get ye gone.
Ride by some other road, Christ speed ye on your way-
I'll hie me home again, but this I'll do alway,
I'll take an oath by God, and all the saints that be,
Or by such hallows all as shall seem best to ye,
That I will hold my peace, and never tell the tale
That ye to face your foe one time for fear did fail."
"Gramercy," quoth Gawain (in sooth ill-pleased was he)
"All good may he receive who wisheth good to me,
That thou would'st silence keep, I well believe of thee,
But, tried be thou, and true, if I should turn me here,
And this thy counsel take, and fly for very fear,
I were a coward knight, excused I might not be,
But at the Chapel Green I'll chance it verily,
With that same man I'll speak, e'en as shall please me well
Be it for weal or woe, as fate the lot may tell-

"So, good Sir Gawain, leave this man alone,
and I pray, for God's sake, get away from this place.
Go by some other way, let Christ speed you on your journey;
I shall go home again, but I will always keep to this:
I'll swear an oath to God, and all the saints there are,
or by any holy thing that seems best to you,
that I will hold my peace, and never tell the story
of how one time you were afraid to face an enemy."
"I thank you," said Gawain (though he was truly annoyed),
"May everyone who wishes me well have good fortune.
I believe that you would keep silent,
but though you are tried and tested, if I turn back here,
and take your advice, and flee out of fear,
I would be a cowardly knight, there would be no excuse;
I'll take my chances at the Green Chapel,
I'll talk with that man there, as I want to,
whether I succeed or fail, fate will decide.

The knave
May well be stern in fight,
Cunning with sword and stave,
Yet God hath mickle might
His servant true to save!"

The scoundrel may well be a good fighter,
skilled with sword and club,
but God has great powers
to save his true servants!"

VII

"By Mary," quoth the squire, "now ye so much have said
That this, your harm, henceforth, to your own count be laid;
Since ye will lose your life I'll hinder not, nor let,
Take ye your spear in hand, on head the helmet set,
And ride adown this road, that by yon rock doth wind,
Till ye the lowest depth of yonder valley find;
A little to the left, on a lawn, shall ye see,
Within that dreary dale, the chapel, verily,
And him, that grisly giant, who shall its keeper be!
Now may God keep ye well, Sir Gawain, noble knight,
For all the gold on earth, I would not, an I might,
In fellowship with ye but one foot further go-"
With that the squire, he turned his horse's head, and so
He spurred him with his heel, and listed not to spare,
But sprang across the lawn, and left the hero there
alone-
"By God," thus quoth Gawain,
I'll neither greet nor groan,
To God's will am I fain,
To Him my need is known!"

"By Mary," said the squire, "you have made
your decision,
and any harm which comes to you is your own
choice;
since you are determined to die I will not stop
you;
take your spear in hand, put your helmet on
your head,
go right down this road, that curves past that
rock,
until you get to the lowest depths of that valley;
on a lawn, a little to the left, you shall see
within that dreary valley, the chapel,
and that horrible giant who is its keeper.
Now may God protect you well, Sir Gawain,
noble knight,
I would not go one foot further in your company
for all the gold on earth."
With that the Squire turned round his horse's
head, and
spurred him with his heels, he didn't spare him,
he charged across the fields, and left the hero
there alone.
"By God," said Gawain,
I shall not wail or moan,
I'm subject to God's will,
he knows what I need!"

VIII

He spurreth Gringalet, and down the path doth ride,
Close 'neath a shelving bank, a grove was at his side;
He rides the rough road through, right down into the dale,

He spurred on Gringalet, and rode down the
path,
alongside a shelving bank, with a wood on his
side;
he followed the rough road on, right down into
the valley,

Then draweth rein awhile, full wild he deemed that vale;
No sign of dwelling-place he see'th anywhere,
On either side the banks rise steeply, bleak and bare,
And rough and rugged rocks, with many a stony peak,
That shuddering shadows cast-the place was ill to seek.
Gawain, he stayed his steed, and cast his glance around,
And changed full oft his cheer, ere he that chapel found.
Nor here 't was seen, nor there, right strange the chance he thought;
But soon, upon a lawn, a lawe his eye hath caught,
A smooth hill by a bank, set close beside a burn,
Where by a ford, the flood, forking, aside doth turn,
E'en as they boiled, within, bubbling, the waters spring-
The knight, he turned the rein, his horse to halt doth bring,
At the lawe lights adown, and to a linden bough
The rein, and his good steed, he maketh fast enow.
Then hies him to the hill, and, walking round about,
He cons what it might be, thereof was he in doubt.
A hole was at the end, and one on either side,
And all with grass o'er-grown, in clumps its form that hide,
'T was hollow all within, e'en as a cavern old,
Or crevice of a crag-nor might its use be told right well-
"Good Lord," quoth the good knight,
"Be this the Green Chapel?
The devil at midnight
Might here his matins tell!"

IX

"I wis," so quoth Gawain, "that wizardry be here,
'T were ill for prayer this place, o'er grown with

then he stopped for a while, the place seemed deserted,
he couldn't see a dwelling place anywhere.
On either side the banks rose steeply, bleak and bare,
and rough and rugged rocks, with many jagged peaks,
cast fearful shadows, it was a dreadful place.
Gawain stopped his horse, and looked around,
and his mood changed often, before he found the chapel.
He couldn't find it anywhere, which he thought very strange;
but soon he saw a little knoll in a glade,
a smooth hill by a bank, right next to a stream,
where the water forked and turned by a ford,
the waters rushed on boiling and bubbling.
The knight pulled on the reins to stop his horse,
and jumped down in the glade, and tied the reins to
a linden tree, making his good horse secure.
Then he went to the hill, and, walking round it,
he saw what it was, which he had been wondering.
There was a hole at the end, and one on either side,
and it was covered over with grass, its sides were earth,
it was hollow inside, like an old cave,
or a crevice in a cliff, and its purpose wasn't clear.
"Good Lord," said the good knight,
is this the Green Chapel?
The devil might hold a service here at midnight!"

"I'm sure," said Gawain, "that there is wizardry here,
this is not a place for prayer, overgrown with

grasses sere,
'T were fitting, did that wight who wraps himself in green
Do his devotions here in devil's wise, I ween!
By my five wits I feel 't is the foul fiend, in truth,
Who here hath given me tryst, my life he seeks, forsooth!
A chapel of mischance, ill fortune may it win,
'T is the most curs'd kirk I e'er set foot within!"
His helmet on his head, his lance gripped fast in hand,
He nighs the rock wherein the dwelling rough doth stand;
Then, from the hill on high, as 't were from out a rock,
On bank beyond the brook, a noise his senses shock;
It clatters thro' the cliffs, as they would cleave in twain,
As one to sharpen scythe on grinding-stone were fain.
Lo! it doth whet and whir as water thro' a mill,
Lo! it doth rush and ring-to hear it was right ill!
Then, "By God," quoth Gawain, "I trow that weapon sheer
They sharpen for that knight who bade me meet him here
this stound.
Let God work as He will,
No help elsewhere were found;
Tho' life be forfeit, still
I blench not for a sound."

rough grass,
I think it shows that that man who dresses in green,
worships the devil here!
All my senses tell me that the foul daemon
will meet me here, he wants my life, I swear!
An evil chapel, it will bring bad luck,
it's the most damnable church I ever stepped inside!"
He put his helmet on his head, gripped his lance tight,
and approached the rock in which the rough dwelling was;
then, from the high hill, as if it came from the rock,
on a bank beyond the stream, he was surprised by noise
which clattered through the cliffs, as if they would split in two,
sounding like someone sharpening a scythe with a whetstone.
There! It scraped and buzzed like water through a mill,
there! It clattered and rang–it was awful to hear!
Then, "By God," said Gawain, "I think they are sharpening
that weapon for the knight who ordered me to meet him here.
Let God's will be done,
there is no other hope;
although I may lose my life,
I will not run away from a sound."

X

With that the goodly knight, he called with voice so bold,
"Who waiteth in this place a tryst with me to hold?
For here is Gawain come, here hath he found his way,
If any wight will win aught, let him come to-day,
Or now, or never, so his need be fitly sped-"
A voice spake from the bank, on high, above his head,

With that the gallant knight called out in a loud voice,
"Who is waiting in this place to meet with me?
Gawain is here, he has found his way,
if any person wants anything from him, let him come today,
now or never, to claim what he wants–"
A voice spoke from the bank above his head,
"Wait, and I will quickly give you what I promised."
The noise still clamoured on, echoing around,

"Stay, and I swift will give that which I promised thee-"
Awhile the clamour rang, still rushing rapidly,
The whetstone whirled awhile, ere he his foe might see,
And then, beneath a crag, forth from a cave he sprung,
And, coming from that hole, a weapon round him swung,
A Danish axe, new dight, wherewith the blow to deal,
Bound to the handle fast was the bright blade of steel,
Four foot long, fitly filed, no less, that blade of might,
And all was wrapped and bound with lace that gleamed full bright;
E'en as before was he in gear of green, that knight-
Green was he face and foot, his hair, his beard's full flow,
But this time on the ground that knight afoot doth go,
Stalking, he held the axe, steel downward, at his side,
Thus to the water wins, and takes it in his stride.
He wades not, with his axe he leaps that water's flow,
And fierce, and bold, bestrides the bent, all white with snow
that day-
Sir Gawain met the knight,
No greeting did he pay,
The other quoth: "Aright
Hast thou kept tryst to-day!"

XI

"Gawain," quoth the Green Knight, "now may God give thee grace,
Welcome art thou, I wis, to this, my dwelling-place;
Thy travel hast thou timed e'en as true man should do-
Thou know'st the forward fast we sware betwixt us two;
This day, a twelve-month past, thy share thereof

the whetstone still spun, before he could see his enemy,
and then, beneath a cliff, he sprang out of a cave,
and, coming from that hole, he swung a weapon around him,
a Viking axe, newly made, to give the blow,
there was a bright blade of steel fixed to the handle,
and that great blade, well sharpened, was at least four foot long,
and everything was wrapped around with bright lace;
just as before he was dressed in green, that knight–
his face and feet were green, his hair, his full beard,
but this time the knight was walking on the ground.
He marched forward, holding the axe head downwards at his side,
and got to the water, and took it in his stride.
He did not wade, with his axe jumped across the stream,
and fierce and bold he marched across the field, which was all white with snow that day.
Sir Gawain met the knight,
he did not give him a greeting,
the other said: "you have kept your appointment well today!"

"Gawain," said the Green Knight, "now may God bless you,
you're welcome to my home;
you have timed your journey as a faithful man should:
you know the bargain that the two of us made;
this day a year ago you had your share,
and this New Year I shall make a proper answer.

didst take,
And I, at this New Year, should fitting answer make.
Here in this dale alone, I trow, we be to-day,
To deal as likes us best, with none to say us nay;
Now doff thy helm from head, thy payment forthwith take,
And with no more debate than I with thee did make
When thou whipped off my head, with but one sweeping blow-”
“Nay, by God,” quoth Gawain, “to whom my life I owe,
Nor greet will I, nor groan, for grief that may befall,
Deal, an thou wilt, the stroke, still will I stand, withal,
Nor bandy words with thee, nor e’er for mercy call-”
Straight there
He bent adown his head,
And shewed his neck all bare,
No sign he gave of dread,
But made as free from care.

XII

Then swift the knight in green made ready for the fray,
And gripped his grim tool fast, as fain Gawain to slay,
With all his body’s force the axe aloft he bare,
A mighty feint he made to deal a death-blow there,
Yea, had he driven adown in wise as he made show
That valiant knight had died beneath the deadly blow.
But as the gisarme fell Gawain, he swerved aside,
E’en as, with fell intent, it did toward him glide;
His shoulders shrank before the sharply gleaming blade,
The other, as he flinched, the axe from falling stayed-
He doth reprove that prince in proud and scornful mood:

We are alone here in this valley today,
to do what we want, with no one to stop us;
take your helmet off your head, take your payment,
and don't argue any more than I did with you
when you whipped off my head with one strong blow."
“No, by God," said Gawain, “to whom I owe my life,
I will not complain or moan about any pain I receive,
make your stroke as you wish, I will face it,
and I will not argue with you, nor call for mercy."
He bent his head at once,
showing his bare neck,
he made no sign of fear,
but behaved as if he hadn't a care.

Then the Green Knight made ready for the fight,
and gripped his grim weapon tight, ready to kill Gawain,
with all his strength he lifted up the axe,
he made a great effort to give a death blow there,
and if he had driven down as he was intending
that brave knight would have died beneath the deadly blow.
But as the axe fell Gawain swerved aside,
even as it headed towards him with evil intent;
his shoulders pulled back from the sharp gleaming blade,
and the other stopped the axe from falling as he flinched.
He reproved that prince with proud and scornful words:
“You are not the Gawain whom men say is so good,
who was never afraid in the mountains or

"Thou art not that Gawain whom men aye deem so good,
Who never waxed afraid, by mountain, or by vale,
Now, ere thou feelest hurt, for fear thine heart doth fail-
Such cowardice in such knight I never thought to know-
I never flinched nor fled, when thou didst aim thy blow,
I made no parleying there, within King Arthur's hall,
My head rolled to my feet, I shewed no fear withal;
And thou, ere harm be done, full sore afraid dost seem-
Henceforward, of us twain the braver men shall deem
me aye-"
"I shrank once," quoth Gawain,
"Henceforth thy stroke I'll stay,
Tho' none may set again
The head that falls to-day!"

XIII

"But haste thee, man, I' faith, thy task to end to bring,
Deal me my destiny, make no more dallying,
For I will stand thy stroke, and start no more, I trow,
Till thine axe hitteth me-my word be gage enow!"
"Have at thee!" quoth the knight, and with his axe made play
With wrathful mien and grim, as mad he were alway.
He struck a mighty blow, yet never wound he dealt,
The axe, his hand withheld, ere Gawain harm had felt.
The knight that stroke abode, nor flinched, that hero free,
But stood still as a stone, or stump of ancient tree
That rooted in the ground with hundred roots hath been-

valleys,
now your courage has failed before you even suffered.
I never thought I would see such cowardice in such a knight,
I did not flinch or run away when you aimed your blow,
I did not negotiate, inside King Arthur's hall,
my head fell to my feet, I did not show fear;
and yet you are afraid before anything has happened:
from now on men shall call me the braver of we two."
"I flinched once," said Gawain,
"from now on I shall wait for your blow, even though it means that
my head will be lost!"

"But hurry, man, get on with your task,
give me my destiny, don't waste any more time,
I will wait for your blow, and I promise I shan't flinch,
until the axe strikes: I give you my word!"
"Have at you!" said the knight, and wielded his axe
with an angry grim look, as if he were mad.
He struck a mighty blow, but never gave the wound,
he stopped the axe from falling before Gawain was hurt.
The knight waited for the blow, and did not flinch, that fine hero,
he stood still as a stone, or an ancient tree stump,
fixed to the ground with a hundred roots;
so then the green clothed giant said merrily,
"So, now you have found your courage, I'll give you your blow,
please hold aside your hood which Arthur gave

Right gaily then he quoth, the giant garbed in green,
"So, now thine heart is whole, the stroke I 'll deal this tide,
Thine hood, that Arthur gave, I prithee hold aside,
And keep thy neck thus bent, that naught may o'er it fall-"
Gawain was greatly wroth, and grimly spake withal:
"Why talk on thus, Sir Knight? o'er-long thy threats so bold,
I trow me in thine heart misgivings thou dost hold!"
"Forsooth," quoth the Green Knight, "since fierce thy speech alway
I will no longer let thine errand wait its pay but strike
He frowned with lip and brow,
Made feint as he would strike
Who hopes no aid, I trow,
May well such pass mislike.

XIV

Lightly he lifts the axe, and lo! it falleth fair,
The sharp blade somewhat bit into the neck so bare;
But, tho' he swiftly struck, he hurt him no whit more
Save only on that side where thro' the skin it shore;
E'en to the flesh, I trow, it cut, the blade so good,
And o'er his shoulders ran to earth the crimson blood.
Sir Gawain saw his blood gleam red on the white snow
And swift he sprang aside, more than a spear-length's throw;
With speed his helmet good upon his head set fast,
His trusty shield and true, he o'er his shoulders cast,
Drew forth his brand so bright, and fiercely spake alway:
(I trow that in this world he ne'er was half so

you,
and keep your neck bent like this so that nothing can cover it."
Gawain was very angry, and spoke sternly:
"Why talk like this, Sir Knight? Your brave threats are too wordy,
I'm beginning to think that you have doubts about what you're doing!"
"I swear," said the Green Knight, "as your speech is so fierce,
I won't delay your punishment any longer, but strike."
His face frowned,
and he made as if to strike,
and there was no help
which could fight against such anger.

He lifted his axe easily, and it fell straight down,
and the sharp blade cut a little into the bare neck;
but although he struck swiftly, he did not hurt him,
except on the side where it cut through the skin;
that fine blade cut through to the flesh,
and the red blood ran over his shoulders to the earth.
Sir Gawain saw his blood gleam red on the white snow,
and swiftly jumped aside, more than a spear's throw away;
he quickly put on his fine helmet,
and grabbed his strong shield,
drew out his bright sword, and spoke fiercely:
(I don't believe he was ever as happy in his life, since the day he was born)
"Now, man, hold back your blow, don't offer me any more,
I took a blow from your hand without arguing,
and if you try and give me another, I shall pay

gay

Since first, from mother's womb he saw the light of day-)

"Now man, withhold thy blow, and proffer me no more,

A stroke here from thy hand without dispute I bore,

Would'st thou another give, that same I'll here repay,

Give thee as good again, thereto have tryst to-day,

and now-

But one stroke to me falls,

So ran the oath, I trow,

We sware in Arthur's halls,

And therefore guard thee now!"

XV

The Green Knight drew aback, and on his axe did lean,

Setting the shaft to ground, upon the blade so keen,

He looked upon the knight awhile, there, on the land,

Doughty, and void of dread, dauntless doth Gawain stand,

All armed for strife-at heart it pleased him mightily,

Then, with voice loud and clear he speaketh merrily,

Hailing aloud the knight, gaily to him doth say:

"Bold Sir, upon this bent be not so stern to-day,

For none, discourteous, here methinks mishandled thee,

Nor will, save e'en as framed at court in forward free;

I promised thee a stroke, thou hast it at this same,

With that be thou content, I make no further claim.

An such had been my will, a buffet, verily,

Rougher I might have dealt, and so done worse to thee,

Firstly, I menace made with but a feign'd blow,

And harmed thee ne'er a whit; that, I would have thee know,

you back,

give you as good as you give, and so be careful,

the oath we swore in Arthur's hall

was that I was to have one blow,

and so now be on guard!"

The Green Knight drew back, and leaned on his axe,

resting it on the ground, head downwards;

he looked at the knight a while, on the ground,

steadfast and free from fear, Gawain stood dauntless,

armed for the fight–this pleased him very much,

and he spoke merrily in a loud clear voice,

calling to the knight, cheerfully saying to him,

"Brave Sir, don't be so angry about this,

for nobody has treated you with discourtesy,

and they will not, except for the terms of the bargain we made at court;

I promised you a blow, and you have had it,

be happy with that, I don't want to do any more.

If I have wanted I could have given you

a much harsher blow, and done you more harm;

firstly I threatened you with a fake blow,

and didn't harm you at all; that, I want you to know,

was for the bargain we made on the first night,

when you made a promise to me, and kept your promise,

you gave me everything you got, like a good true knight;

and for the next morning another fake was due,

you kissed my sweet wife, and gave me back her kisses;

Was for the forward fast we made in that first night
When thou didst swear me troth, and kept that troth aright,
Thou gav'st me all thy gain, e'en as good knight and true-
Thus for the morrow's morn another feint was due,
Didst kiss my gentle wife, and kisses gave again-
For these two from mine axe two blows I did but feign
this stead-
To true man payment true,
Of that may none have dread,
Then, didst withhold my due,
Therefore thy blood I shed."

XVI

"'T is my weed thou dost wear, that self-same lace of green,
'T was woven by my wife, I know it well, I ween,
Thy kisses all I know, thy ways, thy virtues all,
The wooing of my wife, 't was I who willed it all;
I bade her test thy truth-By God who gave me birth
Thou art the truest knight that ever trode this earth!
As one a pearl doth prize, measured 'gainst pease, tho' white,
So do I hold Gawain above all other knight!
Didst thou a little lack, Sir Knight, in loyalty,
'T was not for woman's love, or aught of villainy,
'T was but for love of life, therefore I blame thee less-"
Awhile Sir Gawain stood, silent, for sorriness,
Right sore aggrieved was he, and angered at that same;
Then all his body's blood rushed to his face in flame,
And all for shame he shrank, while yet the Green Knight spake-
Then in this fashion first lament the knight did

for these two I only made two fake blows:
the true man gets paid truly,
none may fear that,
then, you withheld what you owed me,
and so I shed your blood."

"Those are my clothes you're wearing, that green lace,
it was woven by my wife, I know it well,
I know of your kisses, your ways, your goodness,
my wife's attempts at seduction, it was me who ordered it all;
I told her to test your virtue—by God who made me,
you are the truest knight that ever walked the earth!
As highly as one would value a pearl above a pea,
that's how high I value Gawain above any other knight!
If you were a little lacking in loyalty, Sir Knight,
it was not for a woman's love, or any evil purpose,
it was for your love of life, so I blame you less."
Sir Gawain stood for a while, silent, ashamed,
he was tormented, and angry with himself;
his blood rushed into his face, bright red,
and he shrank with shame, while the Green Knight spoke,
then the knight began to speak sorrowfully;
"Covetousness, damn you, and cowardice,
you bring evil and vice to replace virtue."
With that he grabbed the knot, and loosened the

make;
"Covetousness, accurst be thou, and cowardice,
In virtue's stead ye bring both villainy and vice-"

With that he caught the knot, and loosed the lace so bright,
Giveth the girdle green again to the Green Knight,
"Lo! there the false thing take, a foul fate it befall,
Fear of thy blow, it taught me cowardice withal,
With custom covetous to league me, and thus wrong
Largesse and loyalty, which do to knights belong.
Faulty am I, and false, to fear hath been a prey.
From treachery and untruth is sorrow born alway,
and care-
So here I own to thee
That faithless did I fare;
Take thou thy will of me,
Henceforth I'll be more 'ware!"

XVII

The Green Knight laughed aloud, and spake right merrily,
"Whole am I of the hurt that thou didst deal to me;
Thy misdeeds hast thou shewn, and hast confessed thee clean,
Hast borne the penance sharp of this, mine axe-edge keen,
I hold thee here absolved, and purged as clean this morn
As thou hadst ne'er done wrong since the day thou wert born.
This girdle, hemmed with gold, Sir Knight, I give to thee,
'T is green as this my robe, as thou right well may'st see,
Look thou thereon, Gawain, whenas thou forth dost fare,
Mid many a prince of price, and this for token bear
Of chance midst chivalrous knights, that thou

bright lace,
and gave the green girdle back to the Green Knight,
"There! Take the false thing, may an evil fate befall it,
it's made me cowardly, afraid of your blow,
it made me behave like a greedy man, insulting
generosity and loyalty, which knights must have.
I am at fault, and false, I gave in to fear.
From treachery and lies sorrow always comes:
so I admit to you
that I behaved untruthfully;
do what you want with me,
from now on I'll be more careful!"

The Green Knight laughed aloud, and spoke merrily,
"I'm completely healed from the wound that you gave me;
you have confessed your sins and cleansed yourself,
you have suffered the harsh punishment of my sharp axe,
and I say you are now absolved, you are as guiltless this morning
as if you had never done any wrong since the day you were born.
Sir Knight, I give you this girdle hemmed with gold,
it's as green as my robe, as you can see,
look at it, Gawain, when you go from here,
and mix with many high princes, wear this as a token
to show the chivalrous knights that you stayed here;
and you shall ride home with me this New Year's

didst here abide-
And thou, in this New Year with me shalt homeward ride,
With me in revel spend the remnant of this tide I ween-"
The lord, he held him fast,
Quoth: "Tho' my wife hath been
Your foe, that is well past,
Peace be ye twain between!"

XVIII

"Nay, forsooth," quoth Gawain, he seized his helm full fain,
And set it on his head, and thanked his host again;
"Sad was my sojourning, yet bliss be yours alway,
May He, who ruleth all, right swiftly ye repay.
To her, your comely wife, commend me courteously,
Yea, and that other dame, honoured they both may be
Who thus their knight with craft right skilful did beguile-
And yet small marvel 't is if one, thro' woman's wile
Befooled shall be oft-times, and brought to sorrow sore,
For so was he betrayed, Adam, our sire, of yore,
And Solomon full oft! Delilah swift did bring
Samson unto his fate; and David too, the king,
By Bathsheba ensnared, grief to his lot must fall-
Since women these beguiled 't were profit great withal
An one might love them well, and yet believe them not!
For of all men on earth had these the fairest lot,
All other they excelled 'neath Heaven-if they, God wot,
be mused,
Yielding themselves to wile
Of women, whom they used,
Then, an one me beguile,
I hold me well excused."

Day,
and enjoy the rest of the celebrations with me."
The lord embraced him
and said, "Although my wife has been
your opponent, that is all in the past,
be at peace with each other!"

"No, indeed," said Gawain, picking up his helmet
and putting it on his head, and thanking his host again;
"I have had a sad stay, may happiness always be yours,
May He who rules over everything quickly repay you.
Give my sweet greetings to your lovely wife,
yes, and that other lady, may they both be blessed,
the ones who so cleverly tricked their knight.
But it is no surprise for somebody to be
often fooled by women's tricks, and brought to grief,
for that is how our father Adam was brought low,
and Solomon too, very often! Delilah quickly
brought down Sampson, and David the King also
was ensnared by Bathsheba, bringing him grief;
since women managed to trick these men it's very wise
to love them well, but never trust them!
For these men have the greatest fortune on earth,
they were greater than any others: God knows, if they
could be tricked
by their women
then I excuse myself
from being tricked by one."

XIX

"But for your girdle, good, may God the gift
repay,
I take it of good will; not for its gold alway,
For samite, nor for silk, nor for its pendants fair,
For worship, nor for weal, will I that token
wear;
In sign of this, my sin, the silk I still shall see,
And, riding in renown, reproach me bitterly,
Of this my fault, how flesh is all too frail, and
fain
To yield when sore enticed, and gather to it
stain.
Thus, when for prowess fair in arms I yield to
pride,
I'll look upon this lace, and so more humbly
ride.
But one thing would I pray, an so it please ye
well,
Lord are ye of this land, where I awhile did
dwell
With ye in worship fair-(For this, reward be told
From Him who sits on high, and doth the world
uphold-)
But tell me now your name, no more from ye I
crave-"
"That truly will I tell," so spake that baron
brave:
"Bernlak de Hautdesert, so men me rightly call-
'T is she, Morgain la Faye, who dwelleth in
mine hall,
(Who knoweth many a craft, well versed in
cunning wile,
Mistress of Merlin erst,) doth many a man
beguile,
(And many a druerie dear she dealt with that
same wight,
Who was a skilful clerk, and well he knew each
knight
of fame-)
Morgain, the goddess, she,
So men that lady name,
And none so proud shall be
But she his pride can tame!

XX

"But thank you for the girdle, may God repay
you for the gift,
I take it with pleasure; not for its gold,
or rich material, or its fair decorations,
I shall wear the token piously, not for wealth;
when I am celebrated I will still see the silk
which will remind me of my sin and reprimand
me,
reminding me how frail we humans are, and
likely
to give into temptation, and so sin.
So, when my knightly exploits make me proud,
I will look at this lace, and ride on more humbly.
But there's one thing I'd like, if you don't mind;
you are lord of this land, where I lived for a
while,
worshipping with you (and may you get your
reward for that
from the one who sits on high, and preserves the
world)
but now tell me your name, that's all I want to
know."
"I will tell you truthfully," said the brave baron,
"my true name is Bernlack de Hautdesert,
and the woman who lives in my hall is Morgan
le Fay
(she knows many tricks, she is well tutored in
magic,
having been a mistress of Merlin) who has
tricked many men,
(and she had many passionate bouts with that
man, that
accomplished wizard, whom many knights knew
well)
she is Morgan, the goddess,
that's what men call her,
and there is no one so great
that she can't tame them!"

"She sent me in this guise unto King Arthur's
hall
To test your knightly pride, if it were sooth,
withal,
The fair renown that runs, of this, your Table
Round,
'T was she taught me the craft which ye so
strange have found,
To grieve Gaynore, the queen, and her to death
to fright
Thro' fear of that same man who spake, a
ghastly sight,
Before the table high, with severed head in
hand-
'T is she, that ancient dame ye saw in this my
land,
And she is e'en thine aunt, sister to Arthur true,
Born of Tintagel's dame, whom later Uther
knew,
And gat with her a son, Arthur, our noble king,
Therefore unto thine aunt I would thee
straightway bring,
Make merry in mine house, my men are to thee
fain,
And I wish thee as well, here on my faith,
Gawain,
As any man on earth, for true art thou, and tried-
"
But yet he said him "nay" with him he would
not ride.
They clasp, and kiss again-the other, each
commends
Unto the Prince of Peace, and there they part as
friends
on mould-
To the king's hall, I ween,
Sir Gawain rideth bold,
He gat, that knight in green,
Where'er he would on wold.

XXI
The wild ways of the world Sir Gawain now
must trace
A-horse, of this his life, he now hath gotten
grace;
He harbours oft in house, and oft, I ween,

*"She sent me in this disguise into King Arthur's
hall,
to test your knightly virtues, to see if it was true,
the great reputation of your round table,
it was she who taught me the tricks which you
have found so strange,
to scare Guinevere, the Queen, and to frighten
her to death
with the ghastly sight of the man who spoke
at the high table, with his severed head in his
hands—
that's her, that old lady whom you saw in this
land of mine,
and she is in fact your aunt, sister of the good
Arthur,
born from the lady of Tintagel, whom Uther
later knew,
and conceived a son with her, Arthur, our noble
king,
and so I would like to take you right now to your
aunt,
to celebrate in my house, my men revere you,
and I have as many good wishes for you, I
swear, Gawain,
as for any man on earth, for you are true and
tested."
But still he refused and would not ride with him.
They embraced, and kissed again; each
commended the other
to the Prince of Peace, and they parted as
friends on the earth:
Sir Gawain rode straight
to the Hall of the King,
and the Green Knight went
wherever he wished in the world.*

*And now Sir Gawain had to go through the wild
places of the world
on his horse, now that he had been given grace
in his life;
he often stopped in houses, and often slept*

without,
Oft venture bold, in vale, vanquished in battle
stout,
Such as, at this same time, I care not to recall-
Whole was the hurt he won upon his neck
withal,
And the bright belt of green he ware about him
wound,
Even in baldric's wise, fast at his side 't was
bound;
'Neath his left arm the lace was fastened in a
knot,
This token of his fault he bare with him, I wot.
So cometh he to court, all hale, the knight so
true,
Weal wakened in those halls whenas the
dwellers knew
That good Gawain had come-Methinks they
deemed it gain,
To greet that knight with kiss the king and
queen were fain,
And many a valiant knight would kiss and clasp
him there-
Eager, they tidings ask, How did his venture fare
And he doth truly tell of all his toil and care;
Of the Green Chapel's chance, the fashion of the
knight,
The lady's proffered love, last, of the lace aright
He tells, and on his neck he shews them, as a
brand,
The cut that, for his fault, he won from that
knight's hand
in blame
Grieving, he spake alway,
And groaned for very shame,
The red blood rose, that day,
E'en to his face, like flame.

outside,
he often had great adventures, and triumphed in
battle,
which I won't talk about at this time;
the wound on his neck healed,
and he wore the bright belt of green around him,
like a baldric, tied tight to his side;
beneath his left arm the lace was fastened in a
knot,
which he carried with him as a token of his sin.
So he came to court, and everyone greeted this
true knight,
and there were great celebrations there when
the inhabitants knew
that good Gawain had come; they thought it was
a triumph,
and the King and Queen wanted to greet the
knight with a kiss,
and many brave knights wanted to embrace and
kiss him.
They eagerly asked for news of how his
adventure had gone,
and he told them truthfully of all his efforts and
suffering;
of what happened at the Green Chapel, who the
knight was,
the love the lady offered him, and lastly about
the lace,
and he showed them the wound on his neck,
like a brand, that he had, because of his sin,
taken from the knight.
He spoke in sorrow,
and groaned with shame,
the red blood rose into his face
that day like a flame.

XXII

"Lo! lord," so spake the knight, handling the
lace so fair,
"See here the brand of blame that on my neck I
bear,
Lo! here the harm and loss I to myself have
wrought,
The cowardice covetous in which I there was

"Look, lord!" said the knight, handling the
lovely lace,
"see here is the brand of shame that I carry on
my neck,
see the harm and loss I have caused myself,
the cowardly greed which trapped me,
this sign of unfaithfulness, which caught me;

caught,
This token of untruth, wherein I was held fast;
And I this needs must wear long as my life shall last.
For none may hide his harm, nor may that be undone,
Once caught within a snare the net is ne'er unspun!"
The king, he cheered the knight, the courtiers, with their lord,
Laughed loudly at the tale, and sware with one accord,
That lords and ladies all, of this, the Table Round,
Each of the Brotherhood, should bear, as baldric bound,
About his waist, a band, a badge of green so bright,
This would they fitly wear in honour of that knight.
With one accord they sware, those knights so good and true,
And he who bare that badge the greater honour knew.
The best book of Romance, in that 't is written all,
How in King Arthur's days this venture did befall,
The Brutus books thereof, I trow, shall witness bear-
And since Brutus the bold at first did hither fare,
Whose fathers the assault and siege of Troy did share,
I wis,
Many have been of yore
The ventures such as this,
Christ, who a thorn-crown bore,
Bring us unto His bliss! Amen.

and I must carry this as long as I am alive.
For nobody can hide his wrongs, and they may not be undone,
once you're caught in a trap the net can never be loosened."
The King cheered the knight, and the courtiers laughed
along with their lord at the tale, and also all swore together
that the lords and ladies of the round table,
everyone in the brotherhood, should wear as a baldric,
around his waist, a belt, a badge of bright green,
and they would wear it in honour of that knight.
They also swore together, those good and true knights,
that anyone who carried that sign would be honoured by it.
This story is written in the best book of romance,
of how this happened in the days of King Arthur,
and the histories of Brutus bear witness to this;
since Brutus the brave first came here,
whose fathers took part in the assault and siege of Troy,
there have been many
adventures such as this,
and may Christ, who wore the crown of thorns,
receive us into paradise! Amen.

Made in the USA
Middletown, DE
07 January 2019